TAKE THE HIGH ROAD

D1512707

For Margaret Bisset and Liz Condie of the STV Edinburgh
Production Office, who took "The High Road" right from
the very beginning, when it was little more than a wee,
muddy track . . .

Executive Producer ROBERT LOVE
Producer BRIAN MAHONEY
Scriptwriters DON HOUGHTON
  PETER MAY
  TOM WRIGHT
  WILLIAM ANDREW

TAKE THE HIGH ROAD

Summer's Gloaming

by
Don Houghton

Scottish Television

Copyright © Don Houghton and Scottish Television PLC, 1982
All rights reserved.

This book is published by

SCOTTISH TELEVISION
Cowcaddens
Glasgow G2 3PR

in conjunction with

MAINSTREAM PUBLISHING
25a South West Thistle Street Lane
Edinburgh EH2 1EW

ISBN 0 906391 34 2

No part of this book may be reproduced or transmitted in any form
or by any means without permission in writing from the publisher,
except by a reviewer who wishes to quote brief passages in
connection with a review written for insertion in a magazine,
newspaper or broadcast.

Typeset by Spectrum Printing Company, Edinburgh
Printed and bound by Collins, Glasgow.

Contents

Author's Note

The Scots accent used by the folk of Glendarroch has a lilting, distinct quality to it that is most attractive to the Sassenach ear, rather like that of the West Highlander.

I have not, therefore, tried to embellish the dialogue with too many "apostrophied words" (awa', wi', wha', tho', tak', etc.), nor, I hope, overburdened it with a phonetic attempt to duplicate the words and sounds which are unique to specific areas of Scotland. Instead I have punctuated it, here and there, with a hint of the accent—and no more than that.

If you wish to hear the true beauty and clarity of the dialect, I suggest you listen to actress Marjorie Thomson playing "Grace Lachlan", or Eileen McCallum in her role as "Isabel Blair" in almost any episode of *Take the High Road*. I think every word they utter is crystal clear to anyone who shares our common tongue—be they Englishman, Irishman, Welshman, American, Australian, Canadian, New Zealander—or Scotsman.

D.H.

1

The View from Laird's Vantage

This was her favourite place. Fairytales and fantasies could still be built here undisturbed, undistracted by dull truth.

The scenery unrolled before her in great cascading visions, too spellbinding, too dramatic to be wholly real. Especially now when there was a chiffon of mist blurring the surface of the Loch and another thin veil of it tumbling mutely down the southern slope of Ben Darroch. Especially now when the last golden sparklets of summer were dying away, to be displaced, very gently, by the red, fawn and brown patchwork cloak of autumn. Up in Ardvain the bite was there already and the high-country crofters were putting fires in their grates against the evening chill. For the moment, however, the braes of Ardvain were no more than an undulating wash of grey-purple set against the watercolour sky, no more than a painted backdrop for any fairytale.

Elizabeth Cunningham wondered how often, during the course of her life, she had stood on this spot. She pondered the mathematics of this for a while, allowing the fairytales to fade. She would never see her fiftieth birthday again; there were fifty-two weeks in a year; she estimated that she had walked up here to Laird's Vantage, on average, at least once a week . . . No, wait. More than that, surely? When she was younger she used to ride up here regularly . . . In the holidays, almost every day . . . And when she was tiny her father had brought her here often, usually mounted on his shoulders, to gaze at the view, to gasp at the wonder of it all, sometimes two or three times a week . . . What did that add up to? How many times? One—two—maybe three thousand? *She had been here three thousand times?* That was inconceivable! That was a lot of fairytales.

Laird's Vantage lay some two and a half miles from the heart of the village (say, from Blair's Store) and just under two miles from the front door of Glendarroch House. It was more than a knoll, more than a hillock. It was an eminence, a monticle, a *vantage* point. A gentle, even climb

up—an easy, sloping walk down. A nicely measured
constitutional for all but the most laggardly of Elizabeth's
forebears. From the Vantage they could see, on a clear day,
nearly half of all they had owned. Only the far side of
Ardvain with its heathered vastness, together with the
north-eastern glens, the latter masked by the bulk of Ben
Darroch, were hidden to them. Nearly fifty thousand of
their hundred thousand acres were visible.

It could not have changed that much. Elizabeth's grandfather would have seen little that was out of place. Of
course, the road that ribboned round the curving north
shoreline of the Loch, to form its head, was tarmac'd now,
but it still led to Auchtarne. You couldn't see the little
market town, it was on the far side of the Estate boundary
and hidden behind a foreland, but it was there. He would
have known it was there. Larger, certainly, and uglier than
in her grandfather's day, but he couldn't know that—not if
he was standing here.

The village had altered hardly at all. The cottages had
always looked squat and crouched. Only the kirk's tower
rose to any height above the surrounding roofs, like a fist
clenched heavenward, proclaiming that this was still a
God-fearing community, if not in fact, then certainly to all
outward appearances. There was no Inn or Pub, nor had
there been for generations. A hundred and fifty years ago
Glendarroch had been under the pastoral care of a strict,
fire-eating little Minister who saw Satan lurking in every
nook and cranny. He preached an unbending Calvinistic
Gospel and pledged everlasting damnation on all who
touched demon liquor. Elizabeth's great-great grandfather
lived in mortal fear of him. The existing tavern had been
torn down on his orders. It had never been rebuilt. The
Minister's name was William Robert Amity, known to most
as "Wee Hellfire Calamity", though never in his hearing.
So for the last century and a half there had been no public
hearth for the villagers to congregate about. They had
grown used to this. Instead they met in Glendarroch's only
Store and used it as a natural hub. It was the only
whitewashed building in the village and its brightness,
standing out as it did, from its slate-grey neighbours, drew
the inhabitants like moths to a light. Then, as now, it
stocked everything from a pin to a pick-axe, from a ham to

a haggis. It was then, as now, the fountain of all news, local or national, and the breeding ground for every scrap of gossip, true or slanderous. And in Glendarroch there had always been plenty of both.

From this distance Elizabeth's grandfather would have needed a spyglass to see the changes in Glendarroch House. It was listed as "early Victorian Scottish Baronial", which meant it was not as old as it looked, despite the towers, the turrets and the castellations. It owed more in architectural design to the smaller castles of the Rhineland than it did to the aged, gaunt, fort-like homes of past Scottish Chieftains. Through half-closed eyes you could imagine the House to have a mini fairy-palace quality. It needed to be seen indistinctly, so that its lines were ill-defined and its perspective distorted: then you could imagine a regal grandeur it had never really possessed. That's how Elizabeth, even now, sometimes looked at it. However, the grounds were dishevelled and there was no disguising that. The vast lawns, once manicured by eight under-gardeners, were hurriedly mown by towed cutters. Through that same spyglass you might see the ruts left by tractor wheels. You might also note the blind, uncurtained windows that told of uninhabited rooms and empty corridors. Only Elizabeth's apartment, the Estate offices and some storerooms were in use today. But it needed the spyglass. From this distance the viewer could not know how musty it was down there.

Even so, much was exactly the same. The River Darroch glistened its way down from Ardvain, chattering, twisting, bubbling free, then curling, captive, about the base of Ben Darroch, filtering through the woods below the Vantage, past the Dower House, languidly watering the meadows of the tenant farms, under the old stone bridge, running alongside the village, then to funnel out into the Loch, beside the old jetty—as it had always done, would always do. In some places hurrying excitedly, in other places still, hushed and deep, in pools of clear, solid amber.

To the north-west, when the sun was right, the lowest of the croft cottages could be glimpsed: those of Moncur and McNeil, whose families had grazed sheep up there since long before "Wee Hellfire Calamity" had thumped the oaken pulpit of Glendarroch's church. Far beyond them were the remote homes of the Lachlans, the Stewarts, the Tullochs, the Lockharts, the Shaws and the McNairs. (So far away to the west were the McNairs, a mother and her two middle-aged sons, that they were never seen in Glendarroch or in Auchtarne, but took their supplies from Inveraray, which was closer to them by a mile or two). Theirs was another world, another time. Elizabeth's grandfather would have bridged the gap of years quite easily up there. Except that he would have seen Alistair Shaw aged and arthritic now, not as the slim and subtle athlete-hero who had earned prizes galore at a dozen local Highland Games. And he would have seen Grace Lachlan as an old lady, not as the spry, laughing girl he would have remembered. Grace, who was a Lockhart before Lachlan took her to the altar. Grace who had the prettiest ankles of any lass on the Estate and the boldest eyes in the entire county . . . Grace Lachlan, herself a grandmother now . . .

Mountains, grouse moors, deer dotted braes, sheep scattered glens, cattle strewn meadows, trout rich river, peat, heather, gorse, forest and woodland, loch, crofts, farms, the village and the House—all this was one domain. All this had belonged to one family for hundreds of years. It had been attacked, fought over, ravaged, looted, raped and cleared at various times. It had also been defended ardently, loved, nurtured and cherished. Above all it had endured—held tightly by that one family.

Yet when Elizabeth's father, Sir Logan Peddie, the seventh Baronet, the eleventh Laird of Glendarroch, had brought her, his only child, up here to the Vantage, he had never spread out his arms to encompass it all, had never uttered the time-worn cliché, "All this, my child, will be yours one day". He had never said it—because he knew, even when she was small enough to be carried high on his shoulders, that it never would be.

They had lived well, all the Peddies, even up to this last generation, but the Piper, the dour-faced one who played only laments down in some distant tax office below the Border, had to be paid. There would be Death Duties and Mortgages and Loans Outstanding. There would be Overdue Rates, Income Tax and Super Tax and Overdrafts. The Piper would demand his money. A buyer would have to be found . . .

The inevitable happened. Five years ago the pibroch wailed from the Vantage, down through the mists, across the lochside and along the streets of the village to tell them that Sir Logan Peddie, the last Laird of Glendarroch, had died.

A buyer was found. Langemann International, a Frankfurt based, German multinational. It owned a couple of Banks, three Insurance companies and a Finance House. It marketed a popular toilet soap, a washing powder, a household lavatory scourer and an all-purpose detergent. It had a Plastics division, a frozen food factory and an electrical appliance plant. It distributed a line of well-known soft drinks and several brands of hard liquor. It ran a Road transport business, a fleet of giant oil tankers, three refineries, a string of service stations, a Civil Engineering concern, a construction company, a steel works and it spawned subsidiaries with interests in chemicals, armaments and sporting goods. It was powerful, it had vast resources.

It also dealt in Real Estate. It was one of the few organisations that could buy a hundred thousand acres of Scottish heritage and history for cash, albeit in Deutschmarks.

They had some taxable excess profits to use up. They got Glendarroch for a bargain price. It was a buyers' market.

After the outstanding debts had all been paid there was nothing left for any of the surviving Peddie offspring, though Elizabeth was given a "grace-and-favour" seat on the Board of Glendarroch Estates Limited and a rent-free apartment in the draughty House.

Langemann International had plans for the Estate. They wanted to turn the bulk of it into a pleasure complex. They wanted five-star hotels, golf courses, shooting lodges, fishing, skiing, boating, horse-riding, maybe even a casino and a health farm or two. They thought the crofters' cottages would make quaint and attractive chalets and they drew up plans for a ski-lift that would cut across bleak Ardvain . . .

Then the solid, reliable Deutschmark fluttered a fraction on the European money markets. Langemann International was over-extended. There was a cash flow problem. The

Meier Corporation , also German, also Frankfurt based, also a multinational, but more powerful and with even vaster resources, bought out certain Langemann assets, amongst them—Glendarroch Estates Limited.

Elizabeth remained, the House remained, the Estate stood still for a while. There was a hiatus, whilst Frankfurt contemplated the future fate of a hundred thousand acres of Scottish heritage and history. No one felt comfortable. Crofters and villagers alike wrapped their lives about them like blankets against the unwanted "winds of change" and some looked to Elizabeth, as the old Laird's last surviving kin, to guide them through the squalls.

But Elizabeth had little power. She was Meier's "Resident Director", though it gave her very little authority. She could advise, but not decide, suggest but not direct. Since her marriage to Peter Cunningham, an Edinburgh Advocate, she had forfeited the mystique and influence of the Peddie name. Following her quiet divorce from him some years later, she lost the benefit of his masculine presence in a male dominated environment. The traditionalists thought of her as the "Lady Laird", others only as a "Lady Bountiful" who donated generously to Good Causes and presided over village fund-raising schemes, a ready-made "Opener of Fetes" and a professional Committee Chairwoman. And some thought of her as an elegant but useless anachronism who had survived from Times Past, but had no proper place in the Present.

Two foreign owners, in quick succession, had disrupted the known pattern and widened the chasm between the old and the new to a far greater degree than marching years could ever have done.

So she came to Laird's Vantage as often as she could. She made it her haven from reality and continued to weave her fairytales in the stillness that surrounded it. Glendarroch House was a distant golden palace, the Loch was a magical lake from whence a silent barge might glide into sight at any moment, canopied and garlanded, carrying a princess back to her kingdom. Ben Darroch was a mystical mountain and the river flowed with liquid silver. The woods were mounds of emeralds and the heather was a royal purple cloak . . .

However, demons lurked within the mists and Teutonic

dragons roamed close by, for they also inhabited fairytales and Elizabeth could not deny them their existence. Unfortunately, these days, there seemed fewer knights in shining armour to strike down the monsters and "Happy Ever Afters" were a long time coming . . .

It was all very beautiful—and very sad.

At least, that was the view she got from Laird's Vantage.

2

A Smirring on the Glen

"By God, there's a nip out there right enough," said Dougal, as he closed the front door behind him. "I'd say that it was coming all the way down from Brander and Ben Cruachan." He went through the ritual of taking off his boots in the tiny hallway, watched by the eagle eye of his mother, Grace Lachlan. One step inside the croft kitchen with his boots or wellies on and there would be a Cape Wrath blast from her that would make the nip outside seem like a late spring zephyr. "I've heard tell that the summer ends up there before it does anywhere else," he went on as he put his feet into his battered felt slippers and padded into the room.

"I thought you were having your tea with Alice and Bob?" Grace said, ignoring his remarks about the weather. "That's what you said this morning. Did you forget, then? Och, poor Alice will have cooked something nice—and it'll have gone to waste. . ."

"I did not forget, mother," Dougal interrupted. "I was at the Taylors. And I saw wee Donald." Dougal frowned. "The boy was fine," he added.

Donald was Dougal's son, more than two years old now, but living with Alice and Bob Taylor in their cottage farther down the glen. Dougal's wife, Amy, had died in childbirth and Grace's heart was not as strong as it was; fostering him out had been a sad necessity. Though, as fate would have it, perhaps it had been a blessing in disguise for the Taylors. They had discovered that Alice could have no children of her own.

"Alice invited you for tea," insisted Grace. 'Tea', up in Ardvain, was usually a mammoth evening meal. "What happened?"

Dougal sighed and sat down in his armchair by the fireplace. He stared at the carefully laid logs and wished that the night was upon them so that he could set a match to the kindling beneath. He loved to gaze at the dancing flames and feel the warmth of the fire glow over him. Another hour would have to pass before his mother would allow it to be lit. "They were quarrelling again," he said quietly. "Alice and Bob."

Grace turned back to the stove, closed her eyes and murmured a soft, "Oh, dear."

"Alice again, mother. I have to be fair."

"What was it this time?"

Dougal shrugged. "Och, just this and that. Picky wee things, you know. But by the time I went they were at it hammer-and-tongs. I don't think they noticed me leave."

"It's so unlike Alice." And Grace shook her head in disbelief. "Did it start Donald greetin'?"

"Alice won't argue in front of the lad. She didna' start-up till he was in his bed and asleep." Dougal sighed again and glanced over to the photo of Amy on the mantle. "I've spoken to Big Morag Stewart. If it gets any worse, mother, she'll take Donald for a wee while: at least until Alice comes back to her senses." Dougal turned to look at the stove and sniffed the air pointedly. "You've got something cooking, eh?"

"If she comes back to her senses," said Grace, regardless. "The lass needs to have another long talk wi' Dr Wallace. It's all still preyin' on her mind. She wanted a baby of her own so badly. The upset of knowing she canna' have one is unbalancing her."

Dougal looked startled. "You don't think she's going out of her head, mother?"

Grace gave her son a scornful glance. "Och, you great daft lumph! Alice? Going out of her head? What are you blethering about? Do you think I'd have our Donald under that roof for one moment if I thought there was anything *really* wrong with Alice?" She rattled a saucepan against the side of the sink needlessly. "She's just under a wee bit of strain, that's all. Only to be expected."

Dougal nodded his agreement. "Aye," he said definitely. "Aye, only to be expected." He looked over his shoulder at the stove again, longingly. "I've not eaten, mother. You *do* have something cooking, don't you?"

"Only leftovers from last night. Mince and neeps. It would have done me. I'll put on a few more tatties and we'll share it now," she said.

Dougal returned his attention to the cold fireplace and scowled at it. Alice had been cooking a huge loin of pork when the row started. He could recall the lush smell of it now. He liked a bit of pork when there was a nip in the air.

Every muscle in Alice's body was taut and rigid. They were like rods of iron beneath her skin and they ached with the tension. In the bed beside her Bob breathed deeply and evenly—and she resented his ability to sleep. She resented, too, the fact that he was either totally unconscious and at peace, or building dream pictures in his quiescent mind, excluding her, pushing her farther and farther away from him . . .

Dear God, how unreasonable she was becoming. Dear God, how desperately tired she was. Dear God, why *did* she ache so much? Why was her mind in such a perpetual turmoil? Dear God, what was she doing here? Lying here, with the silence pounding in her ears, the darkness heavy on her eyes. . . Lying here, straining, hating . . .

Hating? No, no, surely not? Who could she hate? Bob? Her own kind, gentle man, whom she loved, who loved her, who still laughed and joked and tried so hard to be patient with her, absorbing her anger, her unreasonableness. . .

Hating? Who, then? Wee Donald Lachlan? Her Donald? Bonny laddie that he is. Filling the cottage with his laughter, sometimes his tears, always his energy. . Her own Donald now, whom she loved, who loved her. . . Dear God, no. The boy kept her sane. . .

Hating? Who? What? Ardvain? Aye, well, there was a great blanket of loneliness for you, a scary vastness. . . Respect it, be frightened of it—but you couldn't hate it, could you? The cottage, then? The cottage? Their own place? The home that she and Bob had so lovingly renovated and decorated and made their own. . .

Hating? Who, for pity's sake. . .?

And she knew, of course.

Only herself.

Bob stirred beside her and she felt a tiny quiver of warmth reach through to her from his body, through the ice of her flesh, through to the tingling, raw nerves beneath. Slowly, carefully she turned back the covers, put her feet to the floor and got out of bed. She walked silently to the tiny open window that looked out over the velvet darkness of Ardvain. It was so quiet, so hushed, the stillness reaching far into the gloom of the night as though it went on for ever and ever.

Alice lifted her hands from her side and placed them on her abdomen, one over the other. She pressed there, gently, then made a sort of stirring, circular motion and a soft moan escaped from her lips.

Dear God, dear God, dear God, she had wanted a baby of her own so much. She had needed one desperately. And now they had taken everything away from inside her. She was empty, barren. She was a shell, a painful shell, with useless breasts too tender to touch, useless heart too dead to kindle, useless womb that made of her a neuter, sexless thing, despite what Bob said. He had told her, many times, that it made no difference, that he loved her and wanted her just as much as he ever did. She would not believe him. His insistence angered her and that's when the rows began and the angry words flew from her tongue like vicious bolts that hurt and wounded him so deeply.

She was flawed, like Amy, her sister, Dougal's wife, who died in childbirth bringing wee Donald into the world. Amy had blossomed as the baby grew inside her—only to die and wither as the child took its first breath.

Alice knew she had to have a babe in her arms to make her whole again. It was a consuming passion, more urgent, more compelling than the ecstasies of love-making that she now denied herself. Denied herself and her man, Bob. It was surely an illness. A type of madness, perhaps? Dr Wallace had warned her she would suffer bouts of depression. Depression or madness? Psycho-something-or-other, no doubt? They would have a word for it, just as they had pills for it. But Alice had not taken the pills. She had hidden them in the bottom drawer—in amongst the secret layette she had collected for the baby she would never have.

Depression or madness or hatred. Aye, hatred. But only for herself.

Alice shivered as that chill from Ben Cruachan, where the summer had already ended, cut through her cotton nightie and made cold rivulets of the tears that glistened on her cheeks.

Grass cutting was not one of Archie Menzies' favourite jobs about the place. The lawns around Glendarroch

House seemed to get bigger every year and the tiny towing tractor got smaller and slower and smellier and rattlier and noisier every time he started it up.

Anyway, he wasn't all that certain that grass-cutting was his responsibility. Hadn't been sure about it for years. Seemed to him that it came under the general heading of "agricultural work". He had always said they could get a fair size crop of hay off this lot. Grass-cutting was agricultural work—and Archie was employed on "domestic maintenance". He denied, vehemently, that that meant he was the "odd-job" man. Mind you, mused Archie, as he glanced over his shoulder to check the clattering blades, they took it for granted that he was the "every-job" man—plumber, carpenter, mechanic, electrician, furnaceman, gardener, cleaner, *head-cook and bottle-washer*. . . No, not quite—but they kept on giving him more and more work to do. At least, it seemed that way to him.

He could remember, in the old Laird's time, there was a domestic staff of fourteen for the House. Fourteen. And that wasn't counting the gardeners and the stable staff. All of them working ten hours a day, six and a half days a week. And now he had to do it all on his own! Well, nearly. It had all been so different in the old Laird's heyday. . . Heyday. . . Hay?

Yes, he was sure that grass-cutting, on this scale, was agricultural work. Maybe he would speak to the Factor about it. Or even Mrs Cunningham. One of the men from the Home Farm (except it was known now as Geddes Farm) should be doing it. Archie nodded in self-agreement and shifted his ample backside on the tiny seat beneath him. And another thing, he thought, a man of his proportions could easily develop haemorrhoids sitting for hours on end on this daft, wee, shaking seat! Maybe he ought to talk to Dr Wallace about that. Maybe he could get a medical chit from him. . . Hey, and what about the noise? Not good for a man's eardrums, all that racket. Shouldn't they issue him with yon earmuff things?

If the truth was known. it was the noise of the tractor that worried Archie more than anything else. The sound of the little engine could be heard for some distance. It pinpointed Archie's whereabouts. And Archie didn't like that. It wasn't so much that he was work-shy. It was just that he liked to do things at his own pace and at his own tempo. Unwatched, unsupervised.

He tugged at the steering wheel, swung the nose of the machine round until it was pointing in the direction of the front door of the House and started a new mowing line.

Fiona, Elizabeth Cunningham's daughter, was just coming out. She gave him a cheery wave and got into her car. Archie waved back. By God, he thought, it's not just the lawns around her that got bigger: look at young Fiona's chest, for instance. Aye, and she's not a schoolgirl anymore. Nor had she been for a long time. What was she now? Twenty? Twenty-one? And with a figure to match. Mind you, yon outfit she was wearing this morning left folk in no doubt she was a woman, well and truly. Tight-fitting jumper, tight-fitting jodhpurs and that blonde hair. . Off to Geddes Farm, eh? Off to check her horses? Or check on Alec Geddes? Was it true, he wondered, about young Fiona and Alec Geddes? The man was twice her age, wasn't he? Damn' near, anyway. Archie sighed. Lucky devil—and he didn't give a monkey's cuss about the gossip either, did he? Geddes was as dour as they come, but there must be something about him, eh? Tenant farmer—and the old Laird's granddaughter? It was like something out of D.H. Lawrence, wasn't it?

He watched Fiona's little car accelerate down the drive. She was in a hurry. Off and away, bright and early. Wasn't even eight o'clock yet. How things had changed, eh? A few months back she would have been yelling at him from her bedroom window, telling him it was an unearthly hour to cut the grass and how the devil was she to get her beauty sleep with all that racket going on? She always used to lie in late. Archie could bank on not having to start the mowing till well after ten. Different now. Her horses and ponies had to be fed, mucked out and groomed, ready for the first tourists. He wondered if she was making any money out of her Riding Stable business? Folk were daft to pay for the privilege of getting their backsides rattled on a fractious, trotting hack, when they could get them rattled right here and now for nothing on this blasted tractor. Still, he supposed money was only a secondary consideration over there at Geddes' place.

Archie and the rest of Glendarroch had always thought

Fiona and young Jimmy Blair would pair off permanently. The village had disapproved of that, too, he recalled: Lady Laird's daughter and the local shopkeeper's son. . . D.H. Lawrence again. . . Mrs Cunningham hadn't seemed to mind, though. She let it be known, quite openly, that she liked and approved of Jimmy Blair, regardless of his background. Different story with Geddes. The Lady Laird wasn't too keen on him at all—nor her daughter's associ- ation with him. At least Jimmy and Fiona were about the same age.

Archie tugged at the steering wheel again, made the turn too tight, scowled as the cutters jangled, clattered and clashed behind him and then straightened up and correct- ed, to start another mowing line. . .

At Blair's Store the day was nearly two hours old.

Isabel was always the first to rise and she needed no alarm clock to tell her the time. At six a.m., give or take no more than two minutes, summer, autumn, winter or spring, she would slide quietly from the big double bed, feet instinctively finding her slippers on the floor, arm outstretched for her dressing gown draped over the rail at the bottom of the bed, a glance at Brian snoring gently still, then a careful patter across the floor, open the door, silently down the short corridor and a blissful fifteen minutes total solitude in the bathroom.

By six-thirty she was dressed and rousing first Brian, then Jimmy, with their morning tea. It had to be strong and sweet, identical for the two of them. Always in the same two thin bone-china cups, fine, almost delicate. She had thought, once, how strange that was: a dark-brown "workman's brew", thick and pungent, but it had to be served in best "afternoon-tea" type china. At any other time they would drink tea or coffee out of anything, thick mugs or plastic beakers, even—but that first morning cuppa. . .

Jimmy was invariably the last to come down for his breakfast these days. He liked to spend about twenty minutes lying back in his bed, hands behind his head, staring at the ceiling, contemplating on his work schedule for the day, wondering what unforeseen problems were going to emerge.

Jimmy ran a little aqua-sports enterprise on the loch, mostly water-skiing. He had a good motorboat, good equipment and a couple of reliable lads from Auchtarne to help out. In the season it was a good, profitable enterprise. For the rest of the year it was a dead loss. The weather and the slowly diminishing number of tourist-skiers meant that the season was drawing to a close.

Last year he had Fiona as a partner and she looked after all the paperwork. But now she had the horses and Alec Geddes. He supposed she was happy. He hoped she was: but for her, too, the season was ending. What excuse would she have then to spend so much time up at the Geddes Farm? What would happen when the warmth went out of the nights?

By seven-thirty the morning papers had arrived. By seven-thirty-five Brian and Isabel had started sorting them, ready for the first customers to come and collect them. In the kitchen Jimmy would be frying the bacon and eggs set aside for him by his mother, knob of butter in the pan for his fried bread, kettle coming up to the boil.

It was the same every morning. It was their routine, the Blair ritual, their habit, their pattern. Like starting a car—ignition on, handbrake off, check the road, into first gear, accelerate, pull out, into second. . . And so on. The pattern. It started the day. It got it into gear and moving.

Isabel darted through the back to check that Jimmy wasn't burning anything. She did that every morning, too. "You cook both those eggs, mind, Jimmy," she said. "You get something into that stomach of yours. It'll help keep out the cold."

"Och, away, ma—do you want me to sink like a stone?" But he broke the second egg into the sizzling pan. "Too much food in the stomach can give you cramps, you know?"

"Too little and you'll have no protection against that water."

Jimmy knew better than to attempt to argue against her logic. "What's the weather like?"

"Bright enough now," said Isabel as she quickly cut bread for him: she knew well enough the sort of mess he made out of a fresh loaf. "But your father thinks there'll be a smirring across the loch before the day's out."

A smirring. Jimmy smiled as he heard his mother say the word. It was her, of course, not his father who had used it. She spoke no Gaelic but she loved the true Scottish words. A smirring: neither rain, nor mist, nor fog—but a gentle, velvet quality to the weather, a fine, delicate blur. You found it only north of Carlisle.

"Isabel," his father's voice bellowed from the shop. "Is it the *Express* or *The Scotsman* Mr Paxton takes?"

"Neither," Isabel called back. "It's *The Sun*. And if you looked in the book you'd see. He's been taking it for three years."

"He's a Page Three addict," shouted Jimmy, "like you, Dad."

"Aye," replied his father, "well you ought to see Page Three this morning. Enough to make anyone an addict!"

Isabel smiled. "Och, I'd better get back in there, otherwise he'll be putting the Minister's name on one of the girlie magazines." She made for the door. "You eat *both* those eggs, mind!"

Into first gear, accelerate, pull out, into second. . . Start the pattern, start the day.

Only Sunday was different. Isabel didn't get up until well after seven then (there were still Sunday papers to be sorted) and they took their time over breakfast, all three of them. But for the rest of the week—always the same. That's how they wanted it, that's how they liked it.

That's how it had been ever since Brian Blair had come home from prison.

Difficult, now, to imagine it. That amiable, devoted man out there—a convicted murderer. Yes, that had really rocked Glendarroch to its foundations. That had even struck dumb the gossipers.

Thirteen years ago Jimmy's father, bored with life in the tiny village store, had become entangled with a waitress from the Auchtarne Arms. It was a stupid, emotionless, sordid little adventure that had turned horribly sour and then suddenly climaxed—violently. The girl had black-mailed him, threatened to tell his wife. Unfortunately she knew nothing about the Blair temper. After all, she wasn't a local girl, she had never heard the talk.

In an old garage, just on the outskirts of the village, one night when it was too dark for her to see any danger signals or see the fury in his eyes, she taunted and threatened him for the last time. Brian hit her. She fell back against a workbench and fractured her skull. She was probably dead before she hit the floor.

There was the arrest, the trial, the conviction and then everyone whispered the details for months, for years after. The Court found Brian guilty, sentenced him to life imprisonment and he was taken away.

To everyone's astonishment, Isabel reopened the Store, ignored the stares and whispers, served everyone who came in, quietly and efficiently and settled down to bring up her son, Jimmy. And she waited for Brian to be released. Time rolled on. People got tired of staring and the whispers died away. Her calm determination had defeated them all.

Brian Blair served ten years and then he was released "on licence" into the custody of his wife. The authorities agreed that her home was a good, steady environment. It was a form of parole.

Naturally, the stares and whispers started up again and, for a while, things were very unpleasant. But they weathered that storm, all three of them. They offered the village a firm, united front, Isabel, Jimmy and Brian, supportive of each other and unshakable.

Once again people got tired of staring and the whispers grew silent. Most of them agreed he had paid his debt, most accepted him, others tolerated him and a few loathed, feared and despised him. But only a few. Some went out of their way to make friends and become staunch allies. Amongst these was Elizabeth Cunningham. It helped. The Lady Laird still exerted some influence, especially over the older inhabitants.

That's why the Blairs liked the ordered routine, the secure daily pattern that started the day for them. It spelt normality.

It also explained why Brian drank that strong brew of "institution" tea from a good bone-china cup each morning. For ten years he had drunk from a thick, characterless, chipped "institution" mug. More than anything else he remembered that mug. More than anything else it reminded him of his incarceration and his shame.

Fiona called in to the store for Alec Geddes' morning

paper and sniffed the air appreciatively. "I don't know why it is," she said to Isabel, "but bacon and eggs smell more delicious in here than anywhere else. Jimmy still feeding his face, is he?"

"Oh, I like him to have a good breakfast, you know," said Isabel, smiling.

"He'll get fat—and then all those dollybirds down at the Aqua Sports will lose interest in him." Fiona leaned over the counter and shouted loudly through to the back: "'Morning, James! Go easy on the calories, eh?"

There was a mumbled retort from the kitchen. Jimmy had his mouth full.

"Aye," nodded Brian, soberly, "There's a lot of them down there."

"Calories?" Fiona asked.

"Dollybirds," he said. "Even at this time of the year."

"Well, I wish he'd send some of them up to the stables. We could use the custom. All I had pony trekking yesterday were two old dears with weak bladders, two giggly schoolgirls and a randy Welsh schoolmaster. Hardly worth the effort of tacking-up, really." She gave out with an exaggerated sigh. "Had to stop every half-mile and let the old dears spend a penny. As soon as they disappeared into the bushes, the Welshman got amorous!"

Brian chuckled. "Occupational hazard?" he asked.

"I thought the stables were doing well," said Isabel.

"We were doing fine earlier on. Tailing off now, though. End-of-season trade." Fiona tucked the newspaper under her arm and made for the door. "Only to be expected."

Brian and Isabel watched her go out. Then Isabel frowned and shook her head almost imperceptibly. "There's going to be trouble there, you know," she said.

"Well, it's not as though she needs the money, is it?" And Brian straightened a pile of newspapers in front of him.

"I'm not talking about the stables, Brian."

"No, I didn't think you were."

"It's Fiona and Geddes. The difference in their ages. . ."

"Aye," said Brian, reluctant to pursue the subject.

"There's going to be trouble."

"None of our business."

Isabel lowered her voice a fraction! "It'll upset Jimmy."

"Look, there was never anything between Jimmy and Fiona. . ."

"They grew up together."

"Och, she spent most of her time at yon boarding school in Edinburgh. . ."

"Aye, and in the holidays they were inseparable," insisted Isabel. "And then after they left school. . ."

"They've gone their separate ways now," said Brian.

"That man Geddes will tire of the lass."

"Or she'll tire of him, Isabel."

"It'll break her mother's heart."

Brian shrugged. "Elizabeth Cunningham's heart is made of sterner stuff."

"There's going to be trouble," Isabel repeated.

"Maybe." He waited for a moment before adding: "And then again—maybe not."

"What do you mean?"

"They could get married."

Isabel looked shocked. "Oh, away with you, Brian Blair!"

"Why not? Sophia Loren and that Italian Film Producer. Chaplin and the lass he married. Happens all the time."

"Och, but it's not right!"

"Who says?" Brian asked.

Before she could make any retort to that, Lorna Seton, the Factor's secretary came in. Brian gave her a broad smile and handed over her copy of the *Daily Mail*. "Good morning, Lorna."

"'Morning, Brian. 'Morning Isabel," said Lorna, returning his smile.

"My wife was just saying, before you came in. . ." he began.

Isabel gasped: *"Brian!"*

". . . that there'd be a smirring across the loch before the day is out." Brian kept his face straight. Isabel exhaled with relief. "What do you think, Lorna?"

Lorna was a handsome woman; attractive, certainly, but not beautiful, though she carried her thirty-eight lonely years with a degree of grace. There was a smooth composure about her that labelled her immediately as a secretary. She had, in fact, been married once, many years ago: but it had lasted only a short time. He had been a spendthrift, always in debt, always in trouble. He had deserted her in Glasgow. So she had come back to the area, to her ailing mother in Auchtarne, to the job in Glendarroch. A quiet, efficient, solitary person who wore her aura of loneliness without any degree of despair. It was a kind of privacy, a shield perhaps, as though she had been hurt, imposed upon and wounded. Maybe it had left her vulnerable. Nevertheless, she was well liked in the village. She need not have been short of friends—or lovers. Brian thought that if she let her hair grow, instead of wearing it cropped and too-tidy, she could have been almost beautiful.

"I think," said Lorna, to his question, "we're going to see rain by lunch-time. I can almost guarantee it." She grinned. "I've left my washing out on the line."

Isabel laughed. And Brian stared at Lorna's legs as she hurried from the store.

"Now she can make a man like Geddes a good wife," said Isabel.

"Life's not as simple as that."

"No," she sighed. "No, it's not, is it?" She began to check the change in the till. "Pity, though," she added, quite softly.

Jimmy came storming through from the back and gave his mother a quick kiss on the cheek. "I'm off now," he said. "I haven't time to wash up, but I've stacked my dishes in the sink. Okay, ma?"

"Okay."

He gave his father a thump on the shoulder as he moved past him. "Okay, dad?"

Brian put out a hand and held him in check. "And whilst we're on the subject of Page Three Pin-ups. . ." he said, apropos of nothing.

"Who's on the subject of Page Three Pin-ups?"

". . . Fiona Cunningham says will you send some of your dollybirds up to the stables? She's getting short of customers. Some of your 'groupies' down there might like to take a nature trek on the back of a pony for a change, instead of lying around sunning themselves all day and showing off their bikinis."

"They're skiers, dad. They pay to be on the water. They are not 'groupies'. And horse riding would be too slow for them. Not enough thrills."

"Oh, I can imagine," grinned Brian.

"Stop tormenting the lad," said Isabel.

"It's just jealousy, ma, that's all," Jimmy replied, airily. "Not my fault I'm surrounded by a host of feminine pulchritude. . ."

" 'Pulchritude'? Ah, now there's a word, eh?" said his father. "I'm awful glad you learnt more than plunkin' at school."

"Listen, I'll have you know I take my job very seriously," Jimmy answered, with mock haughtiness. "I have the welfare and safety of dozens of people at heart. It's a grave resonsibility." And Jimmy, too casually, opened the nearest copy of The Sun to page three. "Oh, my God," he whispered. His mother immediately snatched the paper from him and put it under a pile of Telegraphs.

"Mind, I'd take yon job very seriously, too," said Brian, "if I had the welfare of that wee blonde lassie down there to think on. You ken the one I mean, Jimmy? White bikini wi' big red, blotchy flowers on it? And a bonny, pouty wee mouth? Aye, and all that long blonde hair, eh?" Brian stopped there. He had caught a warning glance from Isabel. She trusted him completely now, he knew that. Even so, there was a lingering danger. Memories of things long past that could be lit again by the touchpaper of careless words. He didn't want Isabel to worry needlessly.

"Aye, I know the one you mean, right enough," said Jimmy, a degree quieter. "Bonny face, smashing figure—but a wee bit dumb in the top storey." He glanced at the clock on the wall beyond the counter. "Look at the time," he exclaimed. "Tam and Freddie'll be wanting the keys to the marine shed." He hurried to the door. "I'm away now, ma."

"Will you be in for your tea?" Isabel called.

"Aye, but maybe a wee bit late."

"We'll hold it for you."

"Thanks."

"Have a good day, son," said Brian.

"Aye."

And then Jimmy was outside and walking quickly down the road. He was frowning and suddenly lost in thought, hardly noticing the occasional greeting from passers-by.

White bikini with big red, blotchy flowers on it, long,

long, blonde hair, pouty lips. Yes, he knew the one, right
enough. Knew almost every inch of her! Soft and gentle.
Skin that always seemed cool to the touch, no matter how
hot the day, how tight the embrace. Skin that tanned
evenly to the copper colour of the dying sun reflected on
the loch at the end of the day. Droplets of water on her
shoulders that became glistening, diamond-speckled gems
as she moved. Legs, long, graceful. Hands, delicate, expres-
sive. Hair, a golden cascade. Lips, moist always. Eyes. . .
Only the eyes seemed less than perfect. Too big, perhaps,
if that was possible? Or was it the colour? They should
have been blue. Or green. Instead they were grey. Indefin-
ite grey.

Jeannie Roxburgh. Oh yes, Jimmy knew her, alright.
Great fun at the start—but now she was becoming a
problem.

Archie reckoned another hour and he would have the
lawns finished. It was close to nine o'clock now. He would
be through by ten. Take a long tea-break—and that would
be the morning just about finished, that is, *if* he took an
early lunch. . .

There was Lorna Seton arriving. He gave her a wave,
wiped the imaginary sweat from his brow and looked at
the watch shuddering on his wrist. Ten minutes to nine, on
the dot. You could bet on it. A dead cert. Lorna Seton
would go through that front door at ten-to-nine, every
workday morning, hail or shine. She would be sitting at
her desk, cover already off the typewriter, opening the first
of the incoming envelopes, right on the first chime of nine.
Odds-on favourite. Stake your life on it. He watched her
disappear through the big front door of the House.

Shudder, rattle, clatter-clatter.

No, grass-cutting was not one of Archie's favourite jobs.
Neither was cleaning the drains, nor the windows, nor
servicing the boiler, nor checking the pipes or climbing
ladders. . .

Different when Ken Calder was here, working as the
Estate mechanic. Ken would sometimes help out. For
instance, Ken never minded doing the grass-cutting. Still,
he was alright now, wasn't he? Ken hadn't waited to get the
push when Frankfurt was cutting back on staff. He had got

himself a job at Duff's Garage in Auchtarne. Ironic, though, wasn't it? They still had to call on Ken to service the Estate vehicles, the tractors and the landrovers. Probably cost them twice as much now. Serves them right, thought Archie. Of course, Ken still lived in Glendarroch. Liked it here, he said. All his friends were here—Archie, the Blairs, Lorna. . . Aye, he lodged with Lorna Seton—and that had the tongues wagging for a while, didn't it? Lodged, mind. Respectably, so they said. Paid rent. Even so. . . Old Murdoch and Mrs Mack had a fair old field day. Maybe Lorna wasn't quite as "solitary" as she would have you believe. Still waters, eh?

There was the Factor arriving, Douglas Dunbar. Must be just a few minutes after nine then.

Archie crouched down a little lower and made it look as though he was concentrating on getting the mowing line as straight as a ruler's edge.

So what about Dunbar? Oh, he was alright, mused Archie, as the Factor went inside. Little more than a caretaker for Frankfurt, really. College graduates nowadays —not like the fire-eaters they used to have. Next to the Laird, the Factor was God-Almighty on the Estate. Now they wore tweed jackets from Edinburgh and cavalry twill trousers and English brogues. . .

He swung the tractor round again and saw Elizabeth Cunningham walking towards him across the grass. Archie jabbed at the footbrake just a little too hard and the cutters jangled and screeched behind him. He grinned sheepishly and Elizabeth pulled a face as he came to a halt some yards from her. He switched off the engine and clambered down stiffly from the tractor seat.

"Good morning, Archie."

"'Morning, Mrs Cunningham," he said, brightly. "Thought I'd make a nice early start. Busy day ahead of me. Got a lot to do."

"Yes, I'm sure you have," she answered, unconvinced.

"Grass seems to get thicker every time I start to mow. .."

"You're making ruts as you turn, Archie."

"Am I?" he said. He looked about him for evidence. "Can't see it from here, Mrs Cunningham."

"It's very noticeable from Laird's Vantage."

"Aye, well, maybe from up there. . ."

"Slow down a little as you start your turn," she suggested.

"I already do that, but if I go any slower the damn' thing stalls, Mrs Cunningham. It's too big and clumsy for the job, you see. What we need. . ."

"What we need," echoed Elizabeth, "is a dozen gardeners with a fleet of motor-mowers."

"Or a wee herd of sheep. They'd keep the grass down."

"You've suggested that before."

"I still think it's a good idea."

"Are you going to pay for the fencing, Archie? We'd have to enclose the lawns, wouldn't we? I'd say that would cost about twelve hundred pounds, at least." She smiled. "You know what Frankfurt would say?"

Archie grunted: "Mow the blasted grass."

"Exactly." She looked beyond him to the expanse of lawn, picturing it the way it used to be. "But with a little more care, please," she added.

"Aye," he muttered.

Elizabeth was about to turn away, then remembered what she really wanted Archie for. "Oh, incidentally," she said, "there's a window-pane out at the back. One of those in the old scullery. Frames are all rotten, I think. Perfect invitation for an intruder. It needs boarding up now. Will you see to it, Archie?"

"Right, Mrs Cunningham." But the matter went right out of his head almost immediately.

As Elizabeth had stared at the lawns, Archie's gaze had followed hers. He had seen the mounds of cuttings thrown up by the blades and it had suddenly dawned on him that they all had to be raked up and collected. He would never be through by ten o'clock now. There was another three hours' work here, at least! More likely *four*! He would have no time to himself today at all.

Archie walked back to the small tractor, hoisted himself up on the hateful, bottom-damaging seat, assumed the world-weary expression of an early Christian martyr and turned on the ignition. There was a dull whirring sound, but the engine did not fire.

He remembered, then, that you could never restart it when it was still hot. You had to wait till it cooled down. This was going to add another twenty minutes—more likely twenty five—to his working day. And, worst of all, he could never manage to squeeze a few extra quid for overtime out of the Factor. Seems Frankfurt did not approve of overtime payments. Archie always said they were mean, tight-fisted devils and he regretted, not for the first time, the passing of the last Laird of Glendarroch.

Although he had conveniently forgotten that Sir Logan Peddie had never approved of overtime payments either.

3

Summer's Gloaming

"**S**ound as a bell," said the salesman, enthusiastically. "And you'll nay see a better bargain anywhere in Lanark."

Moira Moncrieff looked at the faded little car doubtfully. It was standing at the end of a long, second row of used vehicles, like a dowdy, diminutive chorus-girl hiding from the all-revealing footlights. A dull blue, slightly dented Mini, admitting, judging by its battered numberplate, to being at least twelve years old. As for the mileage, the mileometer suggested over a hundred thousand, but twice that was probably nearer the mark.

"Lanark's not exactly Coventry, mister," said Moira.

"A good, tidy wee machine, missus. And I'll personally guarantee it for twelve months," he added, knowing full well that his verbal promise didn't mean a thing. He hoped the girl didn't know that, though. "And you'll be able to fold up that pram and fit it into the back without any trouble. That bonny wee baby of yours'll ride like a prince on the back seat. I see you can lift the top away to make it into a carry-cot, eh?" He was grabbing words out of the air, talking fast to distract Moira from examining the rust marks too closely. "Your husband would approve of this motor, I can tell you," he said, smiling broadly.

"I don't have a husband," said Moira.

The salesman was off balance for only a second. He stared at the tiny, sleeping baby in the folding pram. "Ah, well," he chuckled, "they're not obligatory these days, are they?"

"Three hundred," said Moira.

"Eh?"

"I'll give you three hundred quid for the thing."

The salesman frowned and shook his head sadly. "Och, now, you can see the price marked up there, can't you? Three hundred and fifty—and we're cutting it to the bone as it is. . ."

"Three hundred—cash," she said, evenly.

"Done," he snapped. He had a feeling she might be a cash customer right from the start. Women, accompanied

only by a baby, seldom bought cars on their own. This one
was probably running away from home, from the clatter of
neighbours—Lanark could be a small, tight town, when it
wanted. Probably been saving up, with the fiancé, for the
deposit on a house. Then he had chickened-out when he
found she was pregnant. Couldn't face the future on her
own. She would be on her way up to Glasgow to lose
herself. Oh, yes, thought the salesman, that would be the
story.

As it happened, the salesman was totally wrong. There
had been no fiancé, no thought of a deposit for a house
and the father had not "chickened-out"—because Moira
was certain the father had no idea he *was* a father yet! At
least, not of her baby, anyway. That "delight" was still in
store for him.

And Moira was going beyond Glasgow. She was heading for an area called Ardvain, near the village of
Glendarroch, on the other side of Auchtarne. She had a
job finding the place on the map. There didn't seem to be
much there at all, but that's where Lilian's father lived.
She just thought it was about time he met his little baby
daughter.

The salesman took her into the caravan that served as
his office and they went through the paperwork. There
was still five months to go on the M.O.T., she noticed. At
least the last of a long line of owners had taken some care
of the little car. Theoretically it should get her where she
wanted to go. Theoretically.

Moira counted out the three hundred pounds slowly and
noted the greedy look in the salesman's eyes as he stared
at the notes—thirty of them, in tenners. He tried to screw a
few more pounds out of her, moaning about the Insurance
and the cost of transferring the Registration, but Moira
wouldn't listen. She had drawn out all her savings that
morning, £733.17p. By the time she had settled up with
her landlady for the miserable room she rented down by
the mills in New Lanark she would have less than four
hundred pounds to last her till. . . Till when? She had no
idea.

She put the balance of the money back in her spare
handbag and tucked it under the thin carry-cot mattress at
Lilian's feet. The baby slept on, unconcerned.

The salesman knew some hard men in Motherwell: a quick phone call to them and they would be in Lanark before you could blink an eye. The woman had to pick up her suitcase from her lodgings, she'd said—and he had noted the address from her Driving Licence—they could be waiting for her and lift those notes from that carry-cot. .

But he decided against it. There was the car. If anything went wrong the police would trace the connection straight back to him. The salesman had been in trouble with them before. He would just have to be content with selling the two hundred quid banger for a century over its worth. Anyway, the woman looked an independent type. Mid-twenties, dark-haired, good-looking, but with eyes that fired up in a second. She would be no push-over, except, maybe, in bed.

Fortunately the Mini had been out for a test drive earlier in the day, though that prospective buyer had been more discerning or more knowledgeable. He had told the salesman he wouldn't touch the car with a barge-pole. Anyway, by the time Moira got behind the wheel it took only five attempts before the engine coughed into life. The salesman grinned with relief as she drove out of the lot, with the carry-cot wedged safely in the back seat, complete with money and baby, the latter still sleeping peacefully.

An hour later, having paid off her landlady, picked up her suitcase and filled up with petrol (the salesman had left her about four ounces of fuel in the tank), Moira Moncrieff drove onto the M74 Motorway and headed north-west towards Glasgow. She had made arrangements by phone to stay with an old girlfriend in Partick over-night: that would save her a quid or two. Tomorrow she would move off to find Glendarroch and Ardvain.

In the meantime, the car was giving relatively little trouble. The engine was noisy and uneven, but the Mini seemed content to settle for a steady fifty-five miles an hour on the motorway. The brakes were spongy, but gripped if she jabbed at them a couple of times in quick succession and there was no sign of overheating. She had fed Lilian at the service station and the baby had gone back to sleep again, untroubled by the squeaks and the din of the engine.

Moira did not feel at all apprehensive, just quietly

determined. She hoped there wasn't going to be any trouble, but if it came—she would meet it fair and square., head-on. She felt no sense of shame and certainly no anger. She did not intend to blackmail or threaten, but she did want to talk to Lilian's father and perhaps make a few plans for the days ahead. Nothing that would put the poor man under too much obligation, just enough to safeguard the baby's future.

The trouble was that Moira had no idea of the man's surname, nor was she a hundred percent certain that the Christian name he'd given her was the right one.

It was only by luck, and when he was into his fifth dram and chaser, that she had caught the words "Ardvain" and "Glendarroch". She had overheard them quite by accident as he joked with his mates in the bar where she was serving. She was good at remembering place names.

Yes, she had a good memory. She smiled to herself as she felt a tiny tingle play up and down her spine. She could recall, very clearly,almost every moment she had spent in his arms, lost in that big, soft, creaking double bed above the pub.

"Sodden and Tomorrah," intoned Mrs Mack, using her very best doom-laden, sepulchral voice. "Mark my words, Glendarroch is becoming more like Sodden and Tomorrah every day." She sniffed. "And you know what happened to them," she warned.

"Sodom and Gomorrah," Mr Murdoch corrected her, but it was hardly audible.

"Exactly," she boomed, triumphantly. "Destroyed by fire and brimstone!"

"Is that what's going to happen to us?" Isabel asked, trying hard to keep a straight face. She was thankful the shop was empty. Mrs Mack usually held forth when the place was full of customers. Murdoch, seemingly her pale satellite these days, was the only other person there, and, on occasions, he was about as joyless as she was.

"Don't mock, Isabel," said Mrs Mack. She tightened her mouth, until her lips nearly disappeared, and narrowed her eyes. Then she gave an agitated little shrug to her shoulders. "I'm only glad," she went on, tautly, "that Mr Mack never lived to see the evil that is blatantly rampart in this village just now!" She sniffed again. "And the poor Minister totally incapable of fighting it off."

"Or even seeing much of it," muttered Murdoch.

Mrs Mack flashed Murdoch a suspicious look. She was never quite certain about him. There was always a hint of sarcasm there, she thought. "He does his best, I'm sure," she said. Mrs Mack was the Minister's housekeeper and she ruled over the elderly cleric like a school matron, defending him one minute, castigating him the next, sometimes tempering her views with an unsuspected subtlety that would put people off balance.

"I don't see that Glendarroch is *rampantly* evil," said Isabel. "No worse than anywhere else."

"Do you go about with your eyes tightly shut, then?" Mrs Mack was strident in her accusation. "There's Lorna Seton, a divorcee, living openly . . ."

"Blatantly," injected Murdoch.

". . . with Ken Calder. . ."

"Oh, for goodness' sake," said Isabel, impatiently.

" 'Goodness' has nothing to do with it, Isabel!" Mrs Mack snorted.

"He's Lorna's lodger! A lodger, that's all. He gets a room of his own, bed and breakfast—and he pays rent for them. And that's it!"

"How do you know?"

"Aye?" asked Murdoch.

"How do you know any different?"

"Who knows what goes on under that roof?" countered Mrs Mack.

"They're only friends."

"Platonic?"

"Huh," said Murdoch.

"Why not?"

"Temptation!" suggested Mrs Mack, sombrely.

"Aye," nodded Murdoch.

"Och away." And Isabel gave up.

"Then," went on Mrs Mack, "there's little Miss Fiona and Alec Geddes. That's carnal, that is!"

"Is it?" Isabel asked, disinterestedly.

"And God alone knows what happens up in Ardvain these days!" And Mrs Mack gave an involuntary shudder at the very thought.

"And I doubt if it worries Him too much," said Isabel, calmly.

There was an immediate silence as Mrs Mack contemplated whether or not Isabel was guilty of blasphemy with that remark. Murdoch waited patiently for the verdict. Then Mrs Mack decided she wasn't. Magnanimously she decided that it was merely Isabel's opinion—and not a statement. She was glad. She quite liked Isabel. There was a degree of jealousy, of course. Isabel had been elected Chairwoman of the local Guild in preference to her. But, then, that wasn't Isabel's fault, was it? No, in spite of everything Mrs Mack had to admit she quite liked Isabel.

Actually, there was hardly anyone in Glendarroch who disliked Isabel. She was not the type you could hate. She was gentle, motherly, calm—and loyal to a fault. Even when she clashed with people like Mrs Mack they never took umbrage. And when the next customer came into the shop and began criticising Mrs Mack, Isabel would spring to her defence. It was agreed by almost everyone on the Estate that there were too few "Isabels" in this world.

Mrs Mack sighed patiently. She thought it was time for another Biblical quote. She took a lot of comfort from her quotes. The late Mr Mack used them often in times of stress. " 'Who can find a virtuous woman? For her price is far above rubles'," she intoned.

"Rubies," corrected Murdoch.

As usual Mrs Mack ignored him. She dropped her voice a little: "Isabel," she said, "I've got this terrible feeling. It's almost like a pre- pre. . . " She could not find the word.

"Premonition," prompted Murdoch.

"We're going to have to pay for all the wickedness here," she went on. "I've got this feeling that something bad is going to happen. Aye, something dreadful!"

"Fire and brimstone?" Isabel asked, with a broad smile. Sometimes Mrs Mack was quite ludicrous.

"Don't mock, Isabel," she repeated, angrily.

At that moment the shop door opened and Ken Calder came in. Whether or not it was pure coincidence—or part and parcel of Mrs Mack's grim premonition—it was impossible to say, but for Isabel his appearance came as a welcome relief. "Hello Ken," she said.

It was not Mrs Mack's way to make an exit in high
dudgeon. For her, that would be a form of defeat. Or, at
the very least, an indignity. Instead she moved to Ken as
he came to the counter, patted his arm gently, smiled sadly
and said softly: "We're going to have to pay, you know."
Yet another sniff. "We're going to have to pay." Then she
walked slowly to the door and ignored the fact that
Murdoch was staying behind. She went out without a
backward glance.

"Did she think I wasna' going to pay, Isabel?" Ken
Calder asked, perplexed.

"Take no notice, Ken," said Isabel. "She was on about
something else."

Murdoch gave a little sigh of his own and walked over
to the magazine rack to sneak a look at the girlie
magazines and tut-tut over them disapprovingly for a
while.

"It was just a refill for my ballpoint I was after." As
Isabel turned to get it for him, Ken slapped the coins hard
down on the counter for Murdoch to hear. But he was too
engrossed to pay any attention.

"So what are you doing in Glendarroch at this time,
Ken?" Isabel asked as she rang the money on the till.
"Taking the afternoon off, are you?" She gave him his
change.

"No," he replied. "I got a call from the Factor's office.
Seems Archie managed to blow-up the engine of the
mowing tractor. Just started bellowing smoke, he said."

"Fire and brimstone," said Isabel. And she started to
laugh.

Bob Taylor felt his heart lurch with sickening apprehen-
sion. The cottage was empty. It was time for his tea and
there was nothing laid on the table, no smell of cooking,
no kettle boiling, no sign of wee Donald—no sign of Alice.

He called her name loudly, but there was no answer. A
dozen nightmare images flashed through Bob's mind: he
saw Alice having hysterics, threatening Donald—he saw
Alice wandering like a sleepwalker over Ardvain—he saw
her lying, limbs broken, at the base of any one of a
hundred cliffs—he saw her, face down, in any one of a
dozen burns. . .

A couple of months ago he would have paid no heed to her absence. She had been so reliable and careful, but she did like to spend time over at the Lachlans' croft with Grace. He would have assumed she was there, but there would have been a note on the table for him and food ready in the oven.

Alice was different now—ever since she had lost her baby. Morose, irritable, secretive mostly, there were only occasional glimpses of the bonny, patient woman he married these days.

He found her, at last. She was out the back, on the other side of the low stone wall that kept the worst of the winter drifts from their tiny patch of vegetables. Donald was with her, playing quite happily in the gorse, wearing his woolly jumper against the nippy wind that swept down to them from Beinn Drimfern and the high lochs beyond. She was in a summer dress, though, and her face looked pale and pinched with the cold, even though the sun had far to go before its setting.

She was sitting on the ground with her back to the wall, clutching something to her chest. Bob approached quietly, anxious not to startle her. He stopped a yard or two away and jammed his hand up to his mouth to stifle the gasp of anguish that threatened to escape from his lips.

At first he thought it was a live baby she was hugging and crooning to. He could see that it was something wrapped in the white, crochet shawl Morag Stewart had given them—oh, God, how long ago was that now?—but it wasn't alive. It was something that looked grotesque and bizarre and alien.

Alice was staring down, with gentle, loving eyes, at the face of a battered teddy bear! Donald's teddy bear, handed down to him by Dougal—wrapped so carefully in the shawl. She was nursing a thing of worn fur and sawdust, with a sewn-on, black cotton nose and two glass eyes gazing blindly up at her. Nursing it tenderly, rocking it slowly to and fro.

And the front of her dress was unbottoned, as though she had attempted to feed it at her empty breast.

For a long time Bob could not move. He listened, horrified, to her love-filled voice, softly singing a half forgotten Gaelic lullaby to the inanimate bundle in her arms: " 'Balloo baleerie . . . balee . . .' "

And then Donald spotted Bob. He gave out with a happy, excited whoop and charged towards him. "Hush now, Donald," said Alice, without looking up, "you'll wake the baby."

Bob scooped the boy up and whirled him round and round, delighting in the pure normality of Donald's joyous squeals. By the time he put him down, Alice was on her feet. She looked only slightly flustered as she buttoned up her dress, but she would not look at Bob's face.

"Oh, you're home, then?" she said. "Is it that late? Goodness, the time's just run away from me." She handed the shawl-wrapped teddy bear to Donald. "We were playing a game, you see . . . Donald and me . . . I'll have your tea on the table in no time, Bob."

"You'll catch your death of cold in that thin dress, Alice," said Bob, as he lifted Donald over the wall and then helped her. He noticed her hands were icy.

"Oh, it was quite warm earlier on."

"It's past the time for a summer dress."

Her voice became shrill. "I tell you it was quite warm earlier!" She walked towards the cottage. "The sun was hot up here!" He noticed, too, the shame and anger punctuating her words.

"Then I doubt if Donald needed his woolly."

"Are you calling me a liar, now?" She was looking straight into his eyes and Bob saw the tears well up in hers.

"No, Alice," he said, as gently as he could.

She dragged her eyes from his and looked to the ground just beyond him. The teddy bear and the shawl were lying on the grass where Donald had dropped them. Alice looked at the discarded bundle with a terrible longing. She uttered a little moan and suddenly the tears flowed more freely. Donald watched solemnly as she ran into the house followed by Bob, calling to her anxiously.

The boy picked up the teddy bear by its left arm so that it hung from his hand forlornly: for all the world like an E.H. Shepherd illustration of Christopher Robin and Winnie-the-Pooh before bedtime. Then he toddled after them indoors.

The next day Bob took Donald with him to his work. Alice

raised no objection. They had hardly spoken the night
before and no mention was made of the incident by the
wall.

Bob Taylor was not a crofter, though he and Alice had
been given the Finlayson cottage to live in when the old
crofter died. It was, by Ardvain standards anyway, not too
far from the Lachlans' place and that meant that Dougal
and Grace could keep in fairly close touch. After all, even
though Amy was dead, Alice was still considered as
Dougal Lachlan's sister-in-law, and that was considered a
very close kinship up in Ardvain. The only thing that put
Bob Taylor slightly apart from the rest was that he did not
work a croft for a living.

Bob was Glendarroch Estate's Head Water Ghillie,
known, because it was much less of a mouthful, as the
Water Bailiff. Happily, as custodian of the Darroch waters—
the rivers, burns and loch—he had survived the fierce staff
cut-backs ordered by Frankfurt. Even they knew his worth.
The Darroch salmon were internationally famous, the trout
amongst the liveliest in Scotland and much of the credit
for this rested with Bob Taylor. The fishermen who paid a
fortune for a rod on the bank of the River Darroch, felt
reassured as they glimpsed the slim figure of the black-
bearded Water Bailiff striding silently past them. His
invaluable tips were keenly sought, his advice gratefully
hoarded. He knew the spots, knew the pools. He was also
renowned as an expert trout fly-tier and there were
sporting goods shops in Glasgow and Edinburgh that
eagerly bought every Bob Taylor fly he felt inclined to sell.

He loved his work and he knew the worth of his job. He
had been a contented man, but this business with Alice
was beginning to worry him sorely. As always, he sought
advice—or was it solace?—at the Lachlans.

"Dr Wallace warned you it wouldn't be easy, Bob," said
Grace. She had Donald on her knee and was trying to
coax him to drink some milk. Dougal sat at the table
opposite them and remembered that Dr Wallace had told
Grace not to lift the boy. All women were different
creatures, thought Dougal, but he wouldn't dare say it in
his mother's hearing.

"He didn't prepare me for this, though," said Bob.

"Och, just a silly wee fad."

"I thought she'd gone off!"

"Now where would Alice go?" asked Dougal. "The only place she'd have come to would be here."

"If she was ill—if she was distraught, man—she could wander anywhere!" said Bob. "People don't think straight when they're upset, Dougal. They don't act rationally." He sighed. "This is not at all like Alice—you know that!"

"Dr Wallace said she would be alright as long as she took yon pills he prescribed," said Grace. She was as worried as Bob, but she did not intend to let him see that. "They're to calm her down, he said, Och, I've got a lot of faith in Dr Wallace. He saw me through when I was bad, mind."

Bob put his hand in his pocket and brought out a full bottle of capsules. He held them up for Grace and Dougal to see. "She hasn't touched the pills," he said. "I found them in the bottom drawer—together with a whole lot of baby things."

Donald was getting bored with the milk. Grace put it aside and let the boy get down to play on the floor.

"Mother, if she's not taking the medicine . . ." Dougal began.

"The doctor makes his next visit to Ardvain the day after tomorrow," said Grace. "He always calls in here to see me," she grunted, "though I keep telling him it's a waste of his time and mine. He's as regular as clockwork. He manages to get here just as the morning tea is brewing and the tattie scones are cooling. By the time we've finished our chinwag, he's been here nigh on forty minutes. Have Alice call in before eleven."

"Look," said Bob, still worried, "she's not all that keen on Dr Wallace nowadays. . ."

"She'll take note of him—if I'm here."

Dougal nodded. "Aye, she will, for sure." He knew his mother could be very persuasive when she wanted—and no matter how ill Alice might be, she would listen to Grace. Above anyone else, she would listen to Grace.

"Thank you," said Bob. He still looked wretched and depressed.

Grace's face softened. "She'll get over this, Bob. I'm sure of that," she said.

"She wanted that baby so badly." And Bob could see

Alice's face for the moment, joyous, laughing, happy. That
was when Wallace first told her she was pregnant. Then
there was the nightmare of the miscarriage—and Wallace
had to tell her she could never conceive again. Never. She
had to have surgery instead and they took everything
away. There had been precious little joy or laughter or
happiness for either of them after that. "She wanted that
baby so badly," he repeated. "Even though she had our
Donald to care for. It was as though she needed it—
desperately. There's something about Alice and babies. . .
it's a wee bit weird. I don't understand it."

Neither did Dougal and so he shook his head slowly in
sympathy. "Aye, for all the pain and suffering they go
through to bring them into the world. . ." And he looked
down at Donald. "Amy was the same. Och, she was over
the moon when Wallace told her." He shook his head
again, even slower. "And a few months later she was gone
from me."

"But Amy left you your son, Dougal," said Grace. "Alice
has nothing to give Bob. Well, that must be in her mind
somewhere, anyway." She rose and took Donald's un-
finished glass of milk over to the sink. "And there are
some women who just have to feel a bairn in their arms.
They need more than just a man to look after and care
for." Grace stared out of the window. "Dougal, do you not
mind the look that used to come over Alice's face when
wee Donald was just a baby? The way she held him, spoke
to him, sang to him?" Grace closed her eyes and smiled
tenderly. " 'Balloo baleerie . . . Balee. . .' " she crooned,
very softly.

Elizabeth Cunningham paced the floor of the Factor's
office as Dunbar read the letter through for the second
time. The tea Lorna Seton had brought them lay un-
touched in the cups on his desk. For the moment there
was no reaction from Dunbar at all. It was beginning to
infuriate Elizabeth. She had been excited by the contents
of that letter and she wanted some sort of spark from
Douglas Dunbar.

She stopped pacing and confronted him across the desk.
"Well?" she asked.

He laid the letter down and put a hand to his chin, as

though unconsciously checking to make sure he had shaved properly that morning. It was a habit he had when he was thinking hard. "Sir Jeffrey Leighton-Fyffe, eh? Do you know him, Mrs Cunningham?"

"Not personally—no," she said. "But I know *of* him. And I've done some checking around." Elizabeth pulled a chair closer to the front of the desk and sat down on it. She leaned forward. "Old established family. Excellent references. Well respected."

"Pillar of the Scottish Establishment?" Dunbar asked—and he smiled as he said it.

"If you like—yes!" snapped Elizabeth. It was only Dunbar's way of having a gentle dig at her—and her own aristocratic background—but it was just a little irritating sometimes. Especially when there were big and important issues to discuss. "Leighton-Fyffe is an influential member of a dozen Boards. He is also the Vice Chairman of *that* Merchant Bank!" And she pointed to the heading on the letter in front of Dunbar. "And the Financial Adviser for the Pension Fund he mentions, one of the biggest in the country! They are clients of his Bank."

"And Pension Funds are very rich," mused Dunbar.

"Pension Funds are *extremely* rich, Douglas! That particular one measures its assets in several hundreds of millions of pounds! Elizabeth leaned back a fraction. She found she was just a little breathless. She did not want to sound too excited. She rather enjoyed the cool, calm image she knew she projected to the world. It was a safe shield. She waited a second and then added: "And they are looking for major investments."

"In 'land and property', according to Sir Jeffrey Leighton-Fyffe."

"Yes," said Elizabeth. "One of the Pension Funds from down south has just bought an Estate bigger than this in Sutherland. A hundred and twenty thousand acres—and they are not looking for vast profits. Not like our German friends!"

"Do you think Frankfurt would sell out?" asked Dunbar.

"I think they would be delighted to sell out—if the price was right."

"If Leighton-Fyffe bought—then you would just be changing one master for another."

"Yes, I agree," said Elizabeth. "But it would be a Scottish master, Douglas. Scottish money from a Scottish Fund! And they are looking for long term investments. They are not looking to change the whole face of Glendarroch. They don't want to build great ugly hotels or massive marinas by the lochside. They don't want to evict crofters or tenant farmers. They want to sink their money into 'land and property'—they are not seeking fast returns from it. They have no cash flow problems." She was getting breathless again, so she slowed down. "And they are not dictated to by the fickleness of the almighty Deutschmark."

"They don't want to lose money, though, do they?"

"No, of course not. But you always said that Glendarroch, given time, could pay its own way. It would never make a fortune, but it would pay its way, you said. That's all they want, Douglas. That—and the financial asset the land itself represents." Elizabeth spread her hands as though to make the point. "A hundred thousand acres—not premium acres—but *land*. It's a commodity no one can manufacture. All the land there is—is all we've got, all we're ever going to have. That's where the value lies." She picked up the letter and folded it carefully. "They can afford to wait a while to realise on it."

"And in the meantime?" Dunbar asked.

"The whole matter is strictly confidential—and I do mean confidential. They're like Church Commissioners. Very prim, very correct, very discreet. They don't like fuss and they don't like publicity of any sort. Glendarroch will have to keep a very low profile whilst he's here."

Dunbar raised an eyebrow. "Whilst he's here?" he queried.

"Oh, yes," smiled Elizabeth. "His private secretary phoned this afternoon. Sir Jeffrey Leighton-Fyffe is coming to look us over."

"Is he going to stay in Auchtarne?"

"No. He travels with a chauffeur and a housekeeper, a married couple. I've suggested they all stay at the Dower House." Elizabeth rose and walked over to the window behind Dunbar. "I've told Archie to get the place ready. Lorna volunteered to give him a hand after hours. They'll be comfortable there—and he'll have privacy."

Elizabeth gazed out of the window and watched the first

delicate shades of pink begin to tinge the blue of the sky, heralding the gloaming. From here she could see the Laird's Vantage rising like a broad sentinel above the village. She thought she might take a stroll up there this evening, perhaps just before the dusk settled in. There was always a long twilight at this time of the year. She could stand up there and look out over Glendarroch—and weave fairytales again. Perhaps Sir Jeffrey was a knight in shining armour after all? Perhaps he was going to strike down the monsters—and create a "Happy Ever After"? Or was she just being the perennial optimist?

"What do you think?" she asked Dunbar.

"Bloody marvellous," he answered, with quiet enthusiasm, "*if* we can pull it off." He swivelled his chair round to face Elizabeth. "I think I'd sacrifice my own damn' pension to get Frankfurt off my back." He grinned broadly. "Be like a fairytale come true, wouldn't it?"

"Yes, it would," said Elizabeth.

Just visible, where the horizon met Ardvain's unseen silhouette, there was a feathery trace of salmon-coloured cloud creeping towards Glendarroch, but it seemed to be a long way away.

4

Old Friends and New Lovers

"One hundred and sixty-two pounds exactly," said Jeannie Roxburgh—and then signed her name to the cheque with a flourish. "Worth every penny," she added, with a giggle. She tore the cheque from her cheque book and handed it to Jimmy Blair.

"Will you be going home now, Jeannie?" he asked. Jimmy had no qualms about taking the cheque from her. It was the fourth she had written for him. The other three had all been cleared safely. Jeannie Roxburgh might be just a little short on grey matter, but there was certainly no shortage of green stuff in her bank account. Obviously she came from a wealthy family. She had already spent over eight hundred pounds at the Aqua Sports—tuition, hire of the boat and equipment—it all added up.

"Oh, I'm in no hurry," she said.

"Season's ending."

She pouted attractively. "I hate it when things end."

Jimmy laughed. "Well, water-skiing in winter wouldn't be much fun up here, Jeannie."

"Might be," she said. "Has anyone ever tried it?"

"Och, don't be daft." Jimmy went to the open door of his cluttered office and looked out to check that there was no gear left lying around. Only the hardiest of the skiers were still using Loch Darroch; by the end of the month even they would be gone. The water looked so peaceful now, with no churning ski-wakes to disturb its calm. The moored motor-boat lay as still as a rock, its mirrored reflection a perfect inverted image, clearer than the picture of the boat itself. "I've seen this northern end of the loch frozen over in January," Jimmy said.

"Then you should think about hiring out skates," she whispered, right behind him. "Ice hockey is very macho, you know." He felt her arms snake around him, her hands sliding inside his shirt, her head against his back between his shoulder-blades, her whole body pressed up against him.

Jimmy took a deep breath. "Jeannie. . ." he sighed.

"Very macho," she breathed.

For a while Jimmy stood motionless as her fingers dug into his chest. He was just a little scared of the passion he had aroused in her last time. He had to slow it down, talk to her a little first, let it go at his pace. Yes, easy—otherwise he was going to get burnt by her fire. Then it wouldn't be fun anymore, would it? It would get all serious and emotional—and that's not the way a late summer romp should be. Anyway, he needed to know a lot more about her. She'd been around nearly six weeks and she was still an enigma, a fascinating paradox, but Jimmy was not too keen on mysteries. With her looks and her money—she had to be a jet-setter—so what was she doing up here in this remote corner of Scotland? Why wasn't she in the South of France or sunning herself on a Greek island? If daddy was rich, then there were more exotic places than Glendarroch for aqua sports.

"Jeannie," he repeated.

"Yes?"

"You never talk much about yourself."

"So?" She undid a couple of buttons of his shirt, so that it was open now down to his belt.

"Well, it would be nice to know more about you. We've been very—close—you and I, Jeannie. . ."

"Very," she said.

"I don't even know where you live."

"It doesn't matter."

"Or how you spend the rest of your time," insisted Jimmy.

"Bored out of my mind, usually."

"And why you came here?"

She twined one of her long legs about his. "Someone told me about it."

"Who?"

"I forget."

"Are you a poor little rich girl slumming it up in the wilds of Scotland, Jeannie?" He wanted to see if he could make her angry. "Is that it? Out to give the local peasants a treat, eh?"

But she laughed. "Only one of them," she said.

"I don't even know where you're staying."

"Bed and breakfast place out on the Auchtarne road," she shrugged. "Rather nice, really—but the landlady's a dragon." Her hands continued to explore his chest.

In the trees behind the office a bird started an early evensong. Another joined in almost immediately to make it a duet.

"Who are you, Jeannie?" he asked quietly, and turned round to her.

"Your girl, Jimmy," she murmured. "Right through the summer." She raised herself onto her tiptoes and brought her lips to his. She fluttered her mouth over his for a moment, like a moth flirting with a flame. Then she kissed him fiercely and her arms tugged at his shoulders, trying to draw him even closer. He broke away, breathless, and stared at her. Jeannie's eyes were afire, sparks of rapture animating the usual ash-grey colour of her irises. "And long after it's gone—if you want," she said.

"Oh my God!"

She drew back a fraction. "What is it?" she asked, suspiciously.

"We're standing in the open doorway, Jeannie!"

She pouted again, sexily this time. "Then close it."

They moved back inside and Jimmy pushed the door behind him. He heard the Yale lock click into place. Oh, my God, he thought, this is no summer romp, Jimmy-lad. Not for her, anyway.

He tried to remember whether it was this morning, or yesterday morning, he had warned his mother he might be late in for his tea.

The shop was supposed to be shut. Isabel liked to close at about five-thirty, but that rarely happened. People liked to chat and it seemed they always found more to talk about after five. If neither Brian nor Jimmy were home, then Isabel often stayed open until well after six.

Or if it was Big Morag Stewart's day for doing her shopping, as it was today, it could be six-thirty or seven before the 'Open' sign was turned to 'Closed' and the shop door locked.

Big Morag loved 'a bit of a natter', loved to 'catch up on everything'. She would rattle though her 'messages' in less than ten minutes—and then spend at least an hour just talking. Isabel could never resist her.

Morag *was* big—in every way: big boned, big in stature (she was less than an inch off six feet), big voice and big hearted. Certainly big hearted. She was an Ardvain crofter's only daughter—in fact, his only child. That meant she had to be strong and tough and totally self reliant. She could (and did) shepherd and shear with the best of the men, she could carry an ailing ewe across her shoulders for mile after mile, she could build a fence and sink a stake firmly into the ground with no more than four or five sledgehammer blows, she could drive a Landrover up the steep side of Ben Darroch or the heaviest tractor straight down it. And she could work a dog. Even Dougal Lachlan had to admit there were few women who could do that. She could drink dram for dram, pint for pint with the boys—*if* she wanted to: but Morag, stuck in a man's hardy world, craved, under it all, to be a delicate, willowy, helpless girl. Or better still, someone's wife—preferably Dougal Lachlan's. She hid her feelings and her chagrin under a thick armour of broad humour.

". . . Oh, he was alright, I suppose," Morag was saying. "Forestry man, though, and you know what my father thinks about the Forestry."

"Where was he from?"

"He said Glasgow. And that made me suspicious right away."

"Why?"

"Och, Isabel, everyone knows there are no trees in Glasgow!" And Morag gave out with a hearty chuckle. "So how does a Forestry man learn his trade in a concrete jungle? Ask yourself that."

Isabel smiled and shook her head. "Did you see much of him?"

"He was supposed to be working on that new plantation above Scaddie's Chair, but he was hanging around our croft most of the time," said Morag loftily. "Drank more of our tea than we did ourselves. I was feared that my dad would take the shotgun to him at one time."

"But it wasn't just the tea the man was after, eh?" said Isabel, lowering her voice.

Morag leered and winked broadly. "Well, we had no silver in the house for him to steal."

"So?" prompted Isabel.

"He had a canny way with him, I have to admit," And then, almost casually, Morag added: "So, anyway, he asked me if I'd have dinner wi' him in Auchtarne one night."

"Oh, he never!" exclaimed Isabel, gleefully.

"Aye, he did."

"And you accepted, eh?"

"Och, no, of course not."

"What do you mean—'of course not'? You said he had a canny way with him."

Morag leaned an elbow on the counter and drummed her fingers on the surface. "I told him," she said, "that if I was the best he could find to take out to dinner—then he wasna' much of a catch for any lass! And I wouldna' be seen dead wi' any fella that has such lousy taste!"

Isabel exploded with laughter. The story was ludicrous, but knowing Morag, it might just be true. If it was—it was shaded with sadness—but still very funny. There was no way of knowing. "You never said that, Morag," gulped Isabel, breathless with mirth.

"What else would I tell him?" Morag added, with a look of mock surprise. "I had to save my one decent pair of 'going-out' shoes for the Estate ceilidh, didn't I? Dougal Lachlan just refuses to dance wi' me when I'm wearin' ma wellies."

And that sent Isabel into fresh peals of laughter: so it took her a few seconds to realise that a car had pulled up outside the store—a dull blue, slightly dented Mini. She watched as a dark-haired woman leaned over and checked the carry-cot wedged firmly on the back seat.

Then the woman got out of the car and came into the shop. She stood by the door as Isabel quickly dabbed the laughter tears from her eyes and recovered.

"Are you still open?" asked Moira Moncreiff.

"Sort of," said Isabel. "Can I help you?"

Moira came to the counter and exchanged smiles with Big Morag. "Yes, a couple of things, if you don't mind?" She glanced up at the rows of shelves behind Isabel. "Do you sell Gripe Water? It's the one thing I forgot to leave out handy."

Isabel turned and took a bottle from the glass cabinet near the cosmetics. "And travelling gives wee babies the burps, doesn't it?"

Moira searched in her bag for the money. "Och, you should have heard the din she was making a while back."

"A wee daughter then?" asked Morag.

"Aye."

Isabel wrapped the bottle of Gripe Water and handed it to Moira. "And bonny as can be I'll wager, if she takes after her mother."

"Oh, thank you," said Moira, shyly.

"Have you come far?"

"Oh, aye, some distance—but I've done it in easy stages, y'ken. Had to," she sighed. "Yon car took more nursing than my wean."

"There was something else?" asked Isabel.

"Oh, aye," said Moira. "Just information, if you don't mind?"

"Not at all."

"First—could you tell me how to get to a place called Ardvain? And are there any hotels there?" And Moira added hastily: "As cheap as possible."

"You're not thinking of going up to Ardvain this evening, are you?" asked Morag.

"Is it far?"

"Far enough. On top of that—it's a rotten road for anyone who doesn't know it."

"And," added Isabel, "I'm afraid there are no hotels up there."

"Nothing but a few crofts—and a lot of sheep," said Morag. "It's pretty desolate. I should know—I live there."

"Do you know anyone in Ardvain?" asked Isabel.

"How much do I owe you for the Gripe Water?" asked Moira. Isabel didn't know whether she had heard her question—or whether she was evading it.

"Eighty pence. I'm afraid we're a penny or two dearer up here than at the supermarkets." Isabel took the pound note Moira gave her and made the change at the till.

"But you always get a smile with your service," grinned Morag, "and that's worth the extra, I always say."

"Yes," said Moira, "it is indeed."

"Especially if you're on holiday," pursued Morag.

"Aye." Moira thought for a moment. "Maybe you could recommend a good Bed and Breakfast place here in the village?"

"Mrs Macphearson's," said Isabel, without hesitation. "Nice place—clean and she gives you a good breakfast. You'll get in easy at this time of year, most of the tourists have gone. Tell her Isabel Blair sent you. Och, and she loves babies. She'll not charge you extra for it."

"Oh, aye, Molly Macphearson's very reasonable," nodded Morag.

"Bit of a battleaxe, mind, on the outside," said Isabel, "but she's just a softie under it all." She came from behind the counter, took Moira to the open door and pointed up the street. "You'll have come from Auchtarne—so you go back the way you came, back to the Auchtarne Road, less than a mile—and you'll see the house. It's quite big and it has a bonny garden all about it."

"You can't miss it," said Morag. "It has the road to Ardvain right beside it. There's a signpost."

"Thank you."

"The weather should be good tomorrow," went on Morag. "You could make an early start and spend the day in Ardvain. The air's good—even though it's a bit nippy now. But there's not much else up there."

"Aye," said Moira. She smiled at them both. "Thank you again." From the car she could hear that the baby was awake and crying. She hurried to it.

Isabel came back into the shop and noticed that Morag looked very thoughtful. She was staring out of the window, watching the woman getting into her car.

"You don't get too many holidaymakers asking the way to Ardvain, do you?" Isabel said. "Down to Inveraray or up to Oban, but not Ardvain. It's not exactly 'vacationland', is it?"

Morag was still looking at the car, her forehead creased. The woman got the engine to fire at the third attempt. The Mini eased itself away from the front of the shop, made a U-turn at the end and headed back the way it had come, back towards the Auchtarne Road and, presumably, Mrs MacPhearson's Bed and Breakfast place. "Certainly not if you're on your own—wi' a wee baby," agreed Morag, thoughtfully.

"Well, she's not from around here, anyway. I'd say, from her accent, she was either from south of Glasgow—or the Borders." Isabel moved back behind the counter and began checking the till, prior to locking up. "Lowlander, anyway," she said. "Hey, just look at the time, Morag! I'll have to start charging overtime. . ."

"I've seen that woman before," Morag said, quite definitely.

"Oh? Up here?"

"No."

"Where, then? Och, come on, lass, you're not exactly a gadabout, are you? You spend a week preparing for a trip to Auchtarne. . ."

"No, not Auchtarne, either," said Morag. "I've seen her—a while back—but I don't think she had a baby then." She searched her memory, the effort adding more creases to her brow. Then she shrugged and they vanished. "Oh, it's not important. It'll come to me on the drive home."

But Isabel had already got it. The people of Ardvain were not great travellers—but there was one place most of the crofters went, religiously, every year. The crofters, most of the tenant farmers, the ghillies and a fair number of the Estate personnel. "Lanark Market," said Isabel, brightly.

Morag slapped her thigh heartily. "Lanark! That's it!"

"You—and half the population of Glendarroch Estate," said Isabel, ruefully. "The yearly booze-up away from home. God, you should see some of them when they get back. Like something the cat dragged in. What do you lot get up to down there? It's not just buying and selling livestock, that's for sure!"

Big Morag laughed loudly. "You're right, Isabel. And I know where I've seen her. Yon lass wi' the wean is a *barmaid* at the 'Crawford Arms'! That's a pub close to the market. They have rooms there, too. Half the menfolk stay at the 'Crawford'."

They both fell silent for a second or two as they digested that. Then Morag put her hand up to her mouth and her eyes grew big.

"Are you thinking what I'm thinking?" asked Isabel, quite softly.

Morag took her hand away and pulled a face. "It's been a year since we were at the Lanark Market—and she comes up here. . ."

". . . on her own . . ."

". . . with a new baby . . ."

". . .asking the way to Ardvain . . ."

"Oh, my God," whispered Morag. "There'll be at least one worried man up there—as soon as the word gets out!"

"She'd know, surely?" said Isabel. "I mean, who he is?"

"Know? Why? Yon bloody rogues from up there never give their real names to any lass—when they're on the 'toot' in Lanark!" Morag shook her head. "Och, they go wild, Isabel, in the evenings! Wild!" Then suddenly she looked forlorn. "And the only thing in skirts that's safe in town—is me! Drat it!"

There were only three other riders with Fiona and they had been completely unproblematic: a young married couple, who just quietly gasped as every new vista unfolded before them, and a girl from Barnsley, happy to get away from her brash and talkative parents for an hour or two. It had been an almost idyllic hack, not very profitable, of course—Fiona couldn't make much profit on three riders—but very pleasant. They had taken sandwiches and a bottle of chablis in their saddlebags and had picnicked by the riverside, near the old sawmill. The weather had been kind and they had cooled the white wine in the shallows beyond the weir. There had been just enough breeze to keep the flies away and the horses had been well behaved. But now they were getting a bit frisky as they smelt the familiar scents of Geddes Farm and their stables.

Fiona called to her riders to canter. They were in the flat water meadows and the going was easy now right up to the farm.

The farm . . . Alec Geddes. . . How her life had changed since he had leased the place. How quickly he had made her grow from a fractious filly—to this rather strange mature person who ignored the whole world outside the Geddes Farm. . .

The farm. . . Alec Geddes. . . Madness, really, but it didn't matter. Madness, because it was impossible to know what lay in the future. He was dour, often so uncommunicative, so harsh, sometimes downright rude and unpleasant to her—and everyone else. But then, there were moments of absolute joy and tenderness and that's when nothing else mattered. What people said, what people thought, the sniggers, the shocked glares—they didn't matter. She loved Alec. She could suffer it all. Though, whether or not he cared—that was something else again. He didn't give a fig for what people thought or said. But did he give a fig for her?

Fiona did regret, very much, the pain she knew she must be causing her mother. They had had one almighty row—and after that—a kind of armed, well-mannered truce. Alec's name was never mentioned. As long as Fiona lived in the House with her mother, that was the rule, and she would honour it.

What would happen if Alec asked her to leave the House and go and live with him at the farm? She would go of course —but how would that affect her mother? How would Elizabeth Cunningham absorb that huge degree of shame? Her mother had been so strong always. Just about all she knew and all she owned had been taken from her, the Germans had tried to expel her from the Board, it seemed everything conspired to make her leave Glendarroch. But Elizabeth was still there, still Lady of the House—unshiftable. How cruel and ironic it would be if it was Fiona, her daughter, who finally drove her from the place. . .

There was a white convertible TR7 sports car parked, inconsiderately, beside the entrance to the stable yard. The horses shied and lurched nervously as they went past it. Fiona recognised the car. She had seen it parked in the trees near the Aqua Sports—often on its own when the place was supposed to be deserted and the sun had gone down—and there were no lights on in Jimmy's office. She recognised the girl sitting on the bonnet, too, a golden honey blonde with a soft tan highlighting a superb figure. Fiona had seen her more than once down by the lochside, usually clad in the briefest of brief bikinis. She assumed the girl was Jimmy's 'Summer romp'. Maybe, in answer to her request for some customers, he had sent her up to do some riding. Judging by the look of that sports car, the blonde wasn't short of a quid or two, either.

Fiona dismounted and the Barnsley girl took the reins from her and led Tamberlaine, her chestnut, away to a tethering ring by the tack room. Fiona walked over to the white car. Jeannie Roxburgh turned her head slowly and watched her approach.

"Can I help you?" said Fiona evenly. It really was a stupid place to put the car, but she didn't want to flare at the girl in case she was a prospective rider.

"Fiona Cunningham?" asked Jeannie.

"Yes?"

"Ah." Jeannie turned those grey eyes from Fiona and looked out over the water meadows. "I've heard so much about you."

"Really?"

"From Jimmy Blair."

"Oh, I see," said Fiona. "were you wanting to do some riding?"

Jeannie ignored the question. "You and he were in business together once, weren't you? You were his partner in the Aqua Sports."

"That's right."

"You split up?"

"There wasn't enough in it for the two of us." Fiona wondered if the girl really was interested in doing any riding. "I'm sorry, I didn't catch your name, Miss . . .?"

"Not enough in it?" queried Jeannie, turning her attention back to Fiona.

"That's what I said." Fiona was beginning to lose patience and there was an edge creeping into her voice. Jeannie didn't seem to notice.

"Still not enough in it?"

"I don't quite know what you mean?" said Fiona, icily. "Or what it is you want here?"

"No —'partnership'—now, then?"

"No."

"Of any sort?"

"May I ask what you're talking about?" said Fiona.

Jeannie stood up and stretched lazily. She smiled at Fiona, but there was no warmth in it. She opened her car door and got in behind the wheel, whilst Fiona began to fume. Jeannie looked up at her innocently. "I'm sorry. I've been very rude, haven't I? My name's Jeannie Roxburgh. I'm 'dating' Jimmy, as our American cousins would say. And I'm growing very fond of him. Very close." She paused. "I just didn't want to go stepping on anyone else's toes, that's all."

"Well, you're certainly not stepping on mine, Miss Roxburgh. . ." Fiona snapped.

Another voice, a male voice, deep and commanding, cut across her words: "Fiona you ought to set a good example," said Alec Geddes, who had appeared at the other end of the yard. "You ought to be unsaddling Tamberlaine—not passing the time of day with a girl-friend."

"Yes, Alec," said Fiona. And Jeannie wasn't slow in seeing her immediate change of expression. "Right away." She turned back to Jeannie. "Jimmy Blair and I grew up together. We're old friends, that's all. More like brother and sister, if you must know, Miss Roxburgh!"

Jeannie laughed. "Not like you and him, eh?" And she nodded towards Alec Geddes, as he walked over to Tamberlaine.

Still laughing, Jeannie switched on the engine of her TR7, gunned the accelerator, spun the back wheels and roared her powerful little car out of the yard.

Tamberlaine reared at the noise—and Geddes swore.

5

Autumn's Dawning

The next morning was fine, as Morag had predicted, but very cold. There had been a frost and until the sun wrenched itself clear of the horizon the whole of Glendarroch lay under a thin marcasite carpet of it. In the village and by the lochside it had all disappeared by eight-thirty. It stayed for much longer up on Ardvain.

Moira Moncrieff did take Isabel's advice and found Molly MacPhearson's Bed and Breakfast place without any trouble. She was welcomed in by that rather formidable lady and given an attractive, large room at the back, complete with cot—and was charged a rate slightly less than her only other guest at that time, Jeannie Roxburgh. The baby was free: Molly MacPhearson, stiff widow-woman, sometimes a bit dragon-like, adored children. She would probably have paid Moira to have the baby under her roof!

As things turned out, Moira and Lilian did not drive up to Ardvain that morning. The Mini refused to start. Molly phoned through to Duff's Garage in Auchtarne and asked for Ken Calder to come out and have a look at the vehicle for Moira. He arrived about an hour later, driving the Garage tow-truck, with one of the young apprentice mechanics beside him. He examined the little Mini and, to Moira's relief, told her it wasn't serious, but he would have to take the car back to Auchtarne. The battery leads were corroded and thick with verdigris, the engine needed a couple of new gaskets and a securing bolt had sheared through on the starter motor. Petty things, but he would have to take it into the workshop to fix them. He gave her a reasonable quote for the job and Molly MacPhearson knew that if it came from Ken it would be fair. He and the lad hitched up the little car and towed it away. He would have it back to her, Ken promised, later in the day.

So Moira did not start her search of the crofts when she intended. Therefore it was possible that someone up there got a temporary reprieve.

Instead she and Lilian, at Molly's suggestion, made use of the cool sunny day and strolled through the village to the lochside. Molly made up a thermos of tea and a luncheon of chicken and cold meats, tomatoes, salad and a bright red local apple for her. And Moira was still breast-feeding the baby, so if she could find somewhere secluded, that would be no problem. Armed, then, with a supply of fresh nappies, she made up her mind to relax for a while.

Time enough, she thought, to find Lilian's father. She had waited patiently for nearly a year, another day wouldn't matter.

Mrs Mack saw her pushing the small spindly pram down the street and wondered who she was. She was always interested in faces she didn't recognise. This one, thought Mrs Mack, probably belonged to a late-season tourist. She tried to get a glimpse of the baby, but the woman was past her too quickly.

Archie Menzies spotted Moira just as he was coming out of Blair's Store. He gulped, like a fish out of water, turned quickly and went back into the shop, pretending he'd forgotten something, hoping against hope that Moira hadn't seen him. The sudden shock had drained the colour from his face. Isabel thought he was going to be ill.

Grace knew that there was something in the wind, but she didn't know yet what it was. Hamish McNeil had called early and held an urgent, whispered conversation with Dougal out by the front door.

Hamish had seen Big Morag last night on the road outside his croft as she drove back from the village. Almost gleefully she had told him that the dark-haired barmaid from 'The Crawford Arms' in Lanark was now in Glendarroch—with a baby.

A little farther up the road she had come across Robbie Moncur as he walked down from Braedhu, back to his croft. She gave him the news, as well.

She knew it would be all over Ardvain by the next day. Well, at least it would cause a stir, Morag thought—it was a bit of excitement—and they could use some of that up here, couldn't they? Highlight of her summer had been sheep-dipping time.

She had been in two minds whether to call in at the Lachlans on her way home. Grace, she knew, would be intrigued by the news. But then Morag had had an unpleasant thought. Supposing Dougal was the father of that baby? That wasn't so damn' funny. If he was the guilty party she would give him a belt across the ears that would leave him deaf for a week! She had driven back to her croft and brooded about it for hours.

She would love to have had a child by Dougal, she decided. Or by anyone, come to that. But mostly by Dougal. She was still thinking about that when she went to her solitary bed.

Dougal had mumbled something to his mother about going over to Hamish's to help clear a rockfall from one of the burns. He said it was damming up the stream and it would soon flood a lot of his grazing. Others were coming to lend a hand. It was an emergency, Dougal said. And then kept on repeating it, which made Grace suspicious. She assumed it was an excuse for the men to gather for some reason. She wondered why they had to be so secretive about it: just like naughty schoolboys who had broken a window—or pinched apples from the Dower House orchard—and were soon to be found out. Well, she would hear it all eventually. Dougal could no more keep a secret from her—than fly over the moon. He knew it—and Grace knew it.

In the meantime, Grace was far more concerned with Alice's problems. By mid morning she had prepared the tattie scones and they would be ready, cooling, by the time Dr Wallace called.

At ten-thirty, on the dot, his car lumbered up to the Lachlan croft and he saw Grace at her door ready to welcome him in. He could smell the warm aroma of the scones before he was halfway up the path.

"Nice to see a friendly face," Wallace said. "Ardvain seems empty today, Grace."

"Och, most of the menfolk are away to McNeil's, doctor," said Grace, as she ushered him inside. "They'll not even be to their homes for morning tea, so Dougal said. There's been a rockfall across one of Hamish's burns."

Wallace smiled and took a deep appreciative sniff. "All the more of those scones for me, then?"

"I'm expecting Alice and wee Donald over, though."

"Oh, aye," groaned the doctor, gloomily, "and wee

Donald has a monstrous appetite for tattie scones, as I recall."

Grace laughed. "Dinnae fash yoursel', I made an extra batch."

"How is Alice?"

The laughter died and her face dropped. "I'm worried about the lass, doctor." And she told him about the teddy bear incident. He listened carefully, knowing that Grace would not embroider any detail, nor would she bother him with other people's troubles, even though they might be kith and kin, unless the situation needed urgent attention.

"Aye, he said, as she finished, "it affects some women worse than others."

"What about wee Donald?"

"Well, she may hate everybody else—but not the boy. She may even harm herself—and make Bob's life intolerable, but she wouldn't touch Donald."

"Oh, thank God," muttered Grace.

"I really need to get her to see a Psychiatrist. There are a couple of very good men in Glasgow. . ."

"You'd have the very de'il of a job getting her there!"

"Can you help?" asked Wallace.

"You don't have to ask, do you? I can have Donald here for a while—och, you know how much I'd enjoy that—and there's Morag Stewart will help out. She's a big clumsy lass, but she's like an angel wi' bairns." Grace filled the kettle up at the sink. "You talk to Alice about Glasgow. But go canny—she's like a broody mare shying at her own shadow just at present."

"We'll see what we can do."

"Meanwhile. . ." said Grace, turning from the sink and placing a hand on her hip, her face lighter.

"Aye?"

". . . do you want me wi' ma clothes off before—or after—we have oor tea and tattie scones, doctor?"

Wallace grinned broadly. "You're a shameless woman, Grace Lachlan. And if Dougal heard you say that—he'd have a heart attack on the spot!" He chuckled and gave her a wicked look. "Mind you, if you'd said it to me a few years back. . ."

"Huh, you'd've run a mile, so you would!"

Wallace sighed quietly. I'll examine your chest, Grace, *before* I have my tea and scones."

No one at all had turned up at the Aqua Sports that morning, except for Robbie and Alistair, Jimmy's two assistants, and Jeannie, of course, but no other paying customers. Jeannie said she didn't want to ski and Jimmy let the lads have the dinghy so they could go off fishing down the loch. He could call them with the emergency bell if any unexpected skiers arrived. Jimmy announced that he would use the time to catch up on his accounts. Robbie and Alistair looked at Jeannie and exchanged grins. They headed off quickly before he changed his plans.

Jimmy went into his office, sat at his desk and started rummaging though the manilla files spread about on top.

"You mean, you really *are* going to work on your accounts," said Jeannie, watching him from the doorway.

"I really am," said Jimmy. "My paperwork's in a right mess, here."

Jeannie came in and closed the door behind her. She moved to the little table where the tea and coffee mugs were kept and put the electric kettle on. "You need a secretary," she said.

"Can't afford one."

"You might get someone to work very cheaply."

"Who?" asked Jimmy. "Someone like you?"

Jeannie laughed. "I can't type—and I can't add up and get the same answer twice running." She pursed her lips prettily and her eyes went smoky. "But I can make a super cup of coffee—and I have other talents, too."

"Aye," grinned Jimmy, "I know all about them."

"Listen," she said, coming to the desk, "why don't we just take off today? I mean, get into my car—and just take off? Zoom-zoom. There's not all that much traffic on the roads now—especially if we go northwards. We could just drive until we come to somewhere nice for the night. . ."

"Oh, aye," interrupted Jimmy, "and book in as Mr and Mrs Smith, eh? Honeymooners?"

No one cares these days. We could have a lovely meal— and then spend the whole night together—maybe stay on right through till after the weekend." She wrinkled her nose with enthusiasm. "Maybe not get out of bed for days! How about that, Jimmy?"

"How about that?" he said, quietly.

"Well?"

"Oh, come on, Jeannie, be practical. I've got a business to run here—I've work to do." And he pointed to his cluttered desk. "I can't just go gallivantin' off into the wild blue yonder at the drop of a hat. . ."

"You could if you really wanted to." Her expression changed and her lips grew hard.

"No I couldn't."

Behind her the kettle started boiling. She turned away from Jimmy, went back to the little table and jerked the plug out of its socket. "I want you," she said, evenly, "to stay with me tonight. All night, Jimmy."

"Jeannie, I live at home with my folks. . ."

"I want you to stay with me tonight," she repeated.

He rose from behind the desk and went to her. He put his hands on her elbows. "Oh, wait now, Jeannie, don't make these sort of demands, eh? We had a super time, didn't we? A lot of laughs, a lot of fun. . ."

". . . but the 'season's ending'?"

"Aye."

She drew away from him. "And that's that?"

"Maybe. . ." he stopped.

"Go on," she prompted.

"Maybe—it was all getting too serious. . ."

"Maybe I was getting too serious, you mean."

"Look, I'm sorry," said Jimmy.

"About what?" Jeannie shrugged. "Like you said, we had a ball, didn't we? And you were nice and kind and gentle. and it was all lovely, wasn't it?" And there was a touch of sarcasm in her voice. " 'Dumb, bored, dull little girl, bright local lad'. That's all. But it was great, wasn't it?"

"Yes," he answered helplessly.

She stared at him, long and hard, and those grey eyes never blinked. Then the corner of her mouth went up a millimetre or two, giving a hint of a grin. "Never mind, Jimmy, I'll get out of your hair now. No more demands, no complications." She glanced quickly round the room to check that she had left nothing at all behind, nothing of herself. Satisfied about that, she opened the door—and stopped there for a second, perhaps willing Jimmy to call her back inside. But he didn't. "Hey, Jimmy," she said.

"Yes?"

"I hope you have a long, cold winter, my friend." She

laughed, tossed that honey blonde hair defiantly, went out and slammed the door hard behind her.

Jimmy stared at it for a while and realised he had been, unconsciously, holding his breath. He let it out slowly—and shook his head. Then he went back to his desk and sat down heavily. His eyes went up to the door, half expecting it to open again and for Jeannie to come in, half wanting her to.

No, he reasoned, it was better this way. A clean break. Definite. Jeannie would have been a girl hard to shake off—if it had gone on much longer. He smiled to himself. Ah, but while it had lasted—yes, she had really been something else again, hadn't she?

He heard the TR7 roar into life, heard the back wheels spin and then grip as the little sports car zoom-zoomed away.

Jimmy put his hand in his chin and looked at the files on his desk. Maybe, he thought, Jeannie Roxburgh would come back again next summer?

Grace, without too much subtlety, had found an excuse to take Donald out with her to see the chickens, Bob Taylor had rushed off to Hamish McNeil's to help with the rockfall after he had dropped Alice and the boy—so that left her alone in the Lachlan kitchen with Dr Wallace. Alice was under no illusions, she knew the doctor wanted to question her about her behaviour, her 'illness', as she herself termed it.

At first she spoke to him calmly and quietly, answering him without any resentment or even nervousness. To his suggestion that she should go to Glasgow to see a 'specialist' Alice shook her head and said—she didn't think so. She apologised, calmly, quietly, rather like the Alice of old, with that touch of difference, that wisp of shyness. Wallace thought he was making no headway at all.

"After all," Alice said, "if I went to Glasgow—who would look after wee Donald? Bob's out at the crack of dawn—and not home till tea-time—and so helpless, sometimes, about the place. And I couldn't take the lad with me to a place like Glasgow, could I?"

"Grace could have him for a couple of days."

"Doctor, she's not really strong enough, you know. Donald's just a bit of a handful these days. . ."

"Too much for you, too, Alice?" Wallace asked.

"Oh, no, not at all," she reassured him, heartily.

"There's big Morag Stewart."

"Aye, there is." Alice thought for a moment. "She might be able to cope. But Morag has to work her croft. . ."

"Her father could spare her for a couple of days. That's all it would take, you know."

"Just a couple of days?"

"That's all. We need to get an expert's opinion. We need to see what he has to say."

"I don't know," said Alice. "He couldn't make it so that I could have a baby, though, could he? That's all I really want, doctor. Not pills and words and advice. There's nothing wrong with my head." She looked at him steadily. "Or do you think there is?"

"I think you've been under a lot of strain. . ."

"And all the pills in the world won't help that!" Her voice rose. "Will they?"

"Impossible to say. I'm told you didn't take the pills I prescribed."

Her calmness was melting quickly. "I'm alright! Honestly! I am. I just wish people would stop. . . Stop. . ."

"Stop—what, Alice?" asked Wallace, very gently.

"Stop talking about babies!" gasped Alice, irrationally. "All the time!"

"Is that what they do?" Wallace was watching her carefully.

From outside came the sound of Donald's laughter. It seemed to calm her suddenly. She looked at the window. Wallace waited, patiently. "I just get very tired, that's all." Her words were hardly above a whisper.

"Tired?"

"Yes," said Alice. And her thoughts seemed a million miles away, her voice coming to him through some wide void. "So tired. I don't get any sleep, you see. None at all. My eyes just refuse to close—and in the darkness there are awful thoughts drummin' through my mind . . . Awful thoughts . . . Things I would never even dream on . . ." And she fell silent.

"Alice, listen to me, dear," said Wallace and he leaned forward to get her attention. "Listen to me very carefully. I want you to get some rest, y'ken? Some sleep. And I want you to leave wee Donald here—just for a day or so. Leave him with his grannie. You are to go on back to your home, put yourself to bed, take some medicine I'll give you—and just relax. Just get a wee bit of sleep. Then, later, when you're rested—we'll talk about Glasgow, eh?"

"Leave Donald here?" echoed Alice, dully.

"That's what I want you to do," Wallace tried to take her hand, but she pulled it quickly out of his reach. "I'll drive you back to your home and you can look out some things for the lad—just to tide him over. You understand? He'll need a wee bag for his 'jamas, some underclothes, his toothbrush and the like . . ."

Wallace waited for the storm to break, for the hysteria to burst out, the floodgates open—he could understand those symptoms, he expected them. But there was nothing. There was no emotion registering now. She looked empty and hollow.

"He'll need his teddy bear," was all that Alice said.

They sat around the tractor in a morose little group. There *had* been a rockfall across Hamish McNeil's burn, but it was no real hazard. There was certainly no danger of flooding. Hamish and his neighbour, Robbie Moncur, could have cleared the fall inside an hour, using the tractor to tow out the bigger rocks. It did not need seven of the heftiest crofters in Ardvain and the Estate Water Bailiff. In fact, the work had been finished before most of them arrived.

It was still an emergency and this 'council of war' had met to discuss it, even though it had nothing to do with rocks in a little stream. There was Hamish and Robbie, Dougal Lachlan, Willie Tulloch, Jamie Lockhart from beyond Craigie's Dip, the two Shaw brothers, Tam and Bruce, and Bob Taylor, the Water Bailiff, last to arrive.

All had one thing in common, all of them stayed at 'The Crawford Arms' each year when they went to Lanark. All of them knew Moira; but no one, for the moment, was admitting that he knew her better than any of the others. No one, for the moment, was going to ask. The exercise here, beside the now free-flowing burn, was called 'closing the ranks'. They had formulated no plan yet—they were still debating the subject, taking their time. Hamish technically the host, had brought out his old Army waterbottle, full of whisky and this was being handed round solemnly.

"I don't even know Moira's second name," said Robbie Moncur.

"Was it not Montrose?" suggested Willie Tulloch as he handed the waterbottle back to Hamish.

"Monteith," corrected Jamie Lockhart.

"It was Moira Moncrieff," said Dougal Lachlan, evenly. Seven pairs of eyes turned to him thoughtfully. He looked round them quickly. "I've a good head for names."

"Aye, it was Moncrieff," agreed Bob Taylor.

Tam Shaw rubbed his nose—and then stopped as the waterbottle came to him. He took a swig, wiped the back of his mouth with his hand and passed the waterbottle on to his brother, Bruce, next to him. "Alright," said Tam, "so we all stayed at 'The Crawford Arms'—but there were eighteen bedrooms in that place."

"Nearly all of them taken by folk from the Estate," said Hamish.

"And not all crofters, either," Bruce pointed out.

"The Factor did a deal wi' the landlord," Jamie grunted.

"Archie Menzies stayed there last year," said Tam.

"Archie?" said Willie, incredulously. "And yon Moira? Away with you, man!"

"Aye," nodded Tam, "and that dour bugger, Alec Geddes, you mind?"

"Och, he'd too much on his plate wi' yon Fiona Cunningham," shrugged Robbie.

But Bob Taylor shook his head. "Geddes didna know the Cunningham lass all that well then."

"What about the McNair brothers?" suggested Willie. "I canna remember whether they were there or not last year?"

"Aye, they were," said Bruce. The McNair brothers, Hughie and Drew, crofted too far over to the western edge of Ardvain to get to the meeting. Even so, they would probably have heard all about it by now.

"Look," said Bob, firmly, "it doesna matter who stayed at the 'Crawford' or who didn't. That's not important. Everyone from Glendarroch drank there, didn't they? Almost everyone. Moira pulled beer and poured drams for us all. And *she* had a bedroom on the premises!"

"So maybe you didn't have to be staying at the 'Crawford' to be invited up to her room, eh?" said Tam.

"That opens up the field, doesn't it?" grinned his brother.

"Ah, now, hold on," said Dougal. He didn't like the tone of the discussion at all and felt embarrassed at the way they were talking about Moira—as though she was a common harlot. No, she was a kind woman, full of laughter and independence and warmth. The beer came with no collar to it and she never short changed anyone. She treated them all as her special customers at the 'Crawford'. "It's obviously an Ardvain man Moira Moncrieff's looking for," he insisted. "It's obviously someone from up here."

"And probably someone," said Bob, "who never gave her his right name."

"Och, who gives a barmaid his right name, for goodness sakes, man," said Tam. "Anyway, as I recall, Moira called everyone 'Jimmy', didn't she?"

" 'Jimmy', you mind, not 'Jamie'!" emphasised Lockhart.

"Everyone in Glasgow uses the name 'Jimmy'," said Bruce.

"Do you think anyone's going to own up to being the father of that bairn?" asked Hamish.

"Not if he's already married, he's not!" said Willie Tulloch—who was *very* married, with five children under the roof of his croft already.

"She'll know who it is—as soon as she gets up here," said Tam.

"So that's an end to it," said Bob.

"Unless . . ." went on Tam. "Unless . . ." He paused. "You mind Sheila Galbraith?"

"No!" shouted Dougal, angrily. "No, there'll be none o' that!" And indeed most of the men looked away shame-facedly.

Sheila Galbraith had been a tourist from Greenock. She and her girlfriend used to come up to Ardvain each year, hiking and camping. They, too, were kind, full of laughter and warmth. Evidently Sheila was a little too warm, one balmy night, whilst in the arms of Gordon Muir, a young officer cadet, son of an Ardvain ghillie.

The inevitable happened. She became pregnant and asked Gordon to stand by her. He denied that the child

was his—and appealed for help from his father's friends
up on Ardvain. And they did help, some of them. Half a
dozen who felt the need to 'close the ranks'. They said that
they had all slept with Sheila Galbraith, at some time or
another. Her child, they maintained, could belong to any
one of them. Sheila left in disgrace to have her baby in
Greenock. She never did come back to Ardvain or
Glendarroch.

The old Laird was alive then. Somehow he learnt the
truth. He couldn't find the girl to help her—but he sacked
Gordon Muir's father, the ghillie, and evicted the six
crofters immediately. No one heard of any of them again.
No one, thereafter, was very proud of that episode up on
Ardvain.

"Well, I only thought . . ." began Tam.

"Don't let it even cross your mind, Tam!" said Dougal,
the anger bubbling up in him. "That was a foul thing they
did to that lass—and all here know it!"

"Aye," agreed Bob and others nodded.

But Dougal was in full flight now. "What is it we're all on
about, anyway? Moira Moncrieff is going to come up to Ardvain,
whether we want her or not, and she's going to point a finger at
someone up here. She'll name the father of her wee bairn—and
someone's going to have to pay for their fun down in Lanark.
Maybe it's one of us here. Aye, maybe it is. But if he is here—
then it's *his* concern. It's *his* business—and all the daft wee
meetings about it canna change that." He looked round at them
scathingly. Hamish's waterbottle had reached Tam Shaw again,
but he had found that it was empty. He seemed more concerned
about that than Dougal's words. The rest, however, looked
guilty and wretched. Dougal rose to his feet. "If there are
no more rocks to be shifted, Hamish," he said, "I'll be
away." Hamish shook his head and Dougal strode towards
his Landrover. Bob quickly followed him.

"Hey, hold on, Dougal," he said. Dougal slowed and Bob
fell into step beside him. "You fair gave it to 'em, man. By
God, I've not seen you that worked up since one of those
idiot 'Princes Street sportsmen' wounded a stag when you
were culling last year."

"Och, it's just that sometimes we take all this 'loyalty' to
each other too far," said Dougal. Already he was beginning
to simmer down.

"It's good to have loyal neighbours when the snow's above your head outside your croft."

"Aye, I suppose so." Dougal stopped and looked round at the little group by the burn. "They're alright—Hamish and the others . . . It's just the Shaws—especially Tam—he gets under my skin sometimes."

"He never worried you before."

"I never showed it before." Dougal turned to his Landrover and opened the cab door.

"You think it could be him? You think he could have given Moira the bairn?" said Bob.

"Yon 'Wee, sleekit, cow'rin', tim'rous Beastie'? Och, no. Never. Moira Moncrieff'd eat two o' Tam for breakfast— and still call for her porridge!" said Dougal, with conviction.

"Aye, maybe so," agreed Bob. "But then who do you think it is?"

Dougal turned his gaze full on Bob. "Could be you, Bob Taylor." He made it sound like a statement.

Bob did not flinch. "I was thinking it might be you, Dougal Lachlan."

They stared at each other for fully five seconds. Then Dougal gave out with his usual embarrassed scowl, the one he affected when his mother gave him the sharp edge of her tongue, or when the Minister chided him for missing kirk. "Anyway," he said, "I'll bet it's no' Tam Shaw! I'd lay money on that—as a dead certainty!" He got inside the Landrover. "Och, we've more important things to think on, man. There's Alice's health for a start." And Dougal bumped his old Landrover away over the last of Hamish's stunted summer grazing, trailing a belch of blue exhaust smoke behind him.

Dr Wallace drove Alice back to her cottage and gave her a sleeping draught. He collected the things for Donald—and Alice, almost reluctantly, handed him the teddy bear. There was no real fuss. She had been dry-eyed as she took her leave of the lad and she had hardly spoken a word in the car. Wallace promised he would look in the next day— and they would have that long chat about the Glasgow specialist.

It was only after Wallace had left—and in the silence of

her bedroom—that Alice began to weep. She tore great racking sobs from her body and then bit hard on her knuckles to silence the cries. She tried to keep the misery and pain inside herself, allowing no release for her enormous reservoir of loneliness. The vacuum would remain, she was certain, and not even Bob's abundance of love and understanding, she knew, would ever fill it.

She bit into her knuckles until she broke the skin and the blood trickled from her toothmarks. The sight of it seemed to calm her a little. She dabbed at it with a tissue.

She was sleeping quietly and looked serenely peaceful by the time Bob Taylor got home. He tip-toed round the house so as not to wake her and wondered if the rest might not do her more good than all the mind-probing analysis the specialist would probably subject her to.

He wondered, too, as he quite often did these days, whether or not he was to blame for Alice's illness. He felt a surge of guilt and remorse. Was there something more he could have done? Was there something he should not have done? He loved her, he knew that—had he failed to make her believe and understand it? The fact that she could not have a baby of her own really did not matter to him. Not at all. He had told her time and time again. They had Donald, they had each other. Surely she couldn't feel she was failing them in some way? Depriving him of something? My God, having a baby was nothing special, Bob thought, in his typical chauvinistic way. Some women had them at the drop of a hat. Or a man's trews! Like Moira Moncrieff, for instance.

"Well, I've fixed the immediate problems, Mrs Moncrieff," said Ken Calder, staring at the little car doubtfully.

"Miss," Moira corrected him.

"Eh?"

"I'm not married."

"Oh," said Ken, purposely keeping his attention away from Lilian who was gurgling happily in her pram beside them.

The car was parked in Mrs MacPhearson's front drive, having been driven back from the Auchtarne Garage by Ken. He had fixed the gaskets, renewed the battery leads and replaced the securing bolt on the starter motor. He had also recharged the battery and checked over the rest of the car.

"Will it go now ?" asked Moira. She paid him his bill in cash, separating each note carefully.

"Aye, it'll go."

"You don't sound very enthusiastic about it, Mr Calder."

"Well, it's no' exactly a young car, y'ken."

"It's all I could afford," said Moira.

"Aye, so it'll get you about, but treat it gentle." He folded the money and handed her a receipt for it. "Thank you for this."

Moira contemplated for a moment, then she handed Ken a single pound note. "Here, for your trouble."

But Ken shook his head. "Not necessary, Mrs—Miss Moncrieff. I get a reasonable wage. I don't take tips."

Moira shrugged and put the pound back in her handbag. "Please yoursel'. At least I can drop you back to Auchtarne."

"No need," smiled Ken. "I live in Glendarroch and I'm finished for the day. It's just down the road. A comfortable stroll." He was about to take his leave, but he turned back to her again. "Yon wee car o' yours," he said, "it's going to need a bit o' work doing on it before its next M.O.T. Glasgow mechanics'll take you to the cleaners. If you're still around—I'll do it for you and not charge a fortune. Mrs MacPhearson'll vouch for me."

"Aye, well, we'll see," said Moira. "I'm not at all sure how long I'll be here."

"Alright, then, but the offer still holds. Okay?"

"Okay. And thanks."

"Forget it." Just at that moment a gleaming, burgundy-coloured Rolls-Royce glided past them, moving almost silently along the road to Glendarroch. "After all," Ken said, pointing to the limousine, "you may end up driving something like that one of these days." They both stood watching it until its elegant boot disappeared round the bend.

"No," laughed Moira. "Oh, no, it's not really my style."

The Rolls-Royce slowed gently as it approached the turning that led into the centre of the village. It eased round without a murmur.

"Going to be able to find the lane to the Dower House alright, Sawyer?" asked Sir Jeffrey Leighton-Fyffe to his chauffeur-cum-valet, who was driving.

"No problem, sir. It must be this one on the left," said Sawyer. "The instructions from the Factor's office were very simple to follow. Very straightforward."

"Bodes well," said Sir Jeffrey.

They could see Glendarroch House standing aloof from the village, with Laird's Vantage rearing up well behind it like a stranded, greenshrouded mammoth whale. Sawyer turned into the lane that led to the Dower House and Glendarroch disappeared from view as they drove down through a veritable tunnel of trees.

Sir Jeffrey was in a good, relaxed mood. It had been a pleasant drive up from Glasgow, with not too many vehicles sharing the road after Dumbarton. The countryside around here had always attracted him and at this time of the year it was particularly beautiful, with the foliage changing colour almost, one could imagine, as one watched it flowing past. He had also lunched very well at the excellent little inn recommended by Elizabeth Cunningham and where Lorna Seton had rung through to book an unobtrusive table for him. The trout had been superb and the fine half bottle of cold chablis, a Premier Cru, particularly splendid.

"Pretty spot, don't you think, Mrs Sawyer?" asked Sir Jeffrey.

She was sitting in front with her husband. She was Sir Jeffrey's cook-cum-housekeeper. "Ow, it's lover-ly, Sir Jeffrey. It really is," she said, enthusiastically.

In the back Sir Jeffrey winced very slightly. The admirable Mrs Sawyer, who cooked a *Filet de Porc en Croute* like a dream, was a Cockney from Southwark and her accent grated on his Fettes College educated ear.

Then Sawyer spotted the open gates to the Dower House and guided the Rolls through them, drove sedately up the short drive and brought the car to a gentle halt so that the nearside passenger door, where Sir Jeffrey was sitting, was exactly parallel with the front door.

It was not a beautiful house. It was neither very elegant, nor was it very 'notable'. If Glendarroch House was 'Early Victorian Scottish Baronial'—the Dower was 'Mid

Victorian Gothic Rectory'. It might have looked almost austere were it not for the abundance of ivy that clothed its walls, mellowing it with a rich green mantle and hiding the harsh texture of the stone beneath. Like one or two of the maiden aunts who had lived there in years gone by, it boasted generous proportions and a certain stern charm. It was also very comfortable and very peaceful.

The last of the roses were still in evidence in the older flower beds lining the drive by the front door. Elizabeth Cunningham, having chosen her dress with extreme care (it was a full skirted, very feminine, very summery, biscuit and white, cotton affair), was there—cutting a selection of the best of the blooms for the house. She wanted to create the right impression on first greeting Sir Jeffrey. It was planned, of course. A stage-managed effect, but there was a lot at stake. Inside the house there was a bottle of vintage Taittinger champagne, a classic marque, cooling in an ice bucket, with two fluted Waterford glasses on a Georgian silver tray. They were beside the french windows in the lounge, unobtrusively placed on a Louis the Fourteenth *escritoire*, brought over especially that morning from Glendarroch House.

Sawyer opened the car door for Sir Jeffrey and held it for him as he got out. By that time Elizabeth had advanced to meet him. They got their first good look at each other at exactly the same second—and in an instant all their preconceived notions were shattered.

Elizabeth had believed she would find Sir Jeffrey to be a somewhat paunchy, perhaps balding, fussy little fellow with a slightly bulbous, whisky-endowed nose. She was unprepared for the tall, slim, finely groomed man who emerged from the burgundy limousine. He looked most aristocratic—rather in the Continental manner, his bearing —a cross between the Latin charm and vivacity of, say, Vittorio de Sica and the cool elegance of Curt Jurgens. She had carefully researched his background and his career, but he was known to be a retiring, private person—and she had been unable to find any photographs of him. In her mind she had built up an entirely false mental image of him.

Sir Jeffrey had done the same with Elizabeth. Knowing her to be the middle-aged daughter of the late Sir Logan

Peddie, an old-style traditional Laird, he had expected a hearty, toothy, horsey, battleship of a female, all hairy tweeds and woollen stockings. Instead he found this most handsome and attractive woman, who moved with exquisite grace, whose face was perfectly proportioned, whose eyes were animated and fascinatingly bright and whose mouth was generous and appealing.

A moment hiccupped in time whilst they both readjusted. It stayed suspended until Elizabeth plucked it down to earth by offering her hand to him. "Sir Jeffrey," she said. And she smiled as he took it and brought it to his lips.

"Elizabeth Cunningham," he answered.

"Welcome to Glendarroch."

"I'm delighted to be here."

Sawyer opened the boot and he and his wife took the luggage out and carried it into the house.

"Did you have a pleasant trip?" asked Elizabeth.

"Very nice indeed and totally trouble-free."

"Oh, that's good."

"And that place you recommended for lunch," Sir Jeffrey enthused, "excellent." He looked at the white blooms in the crook of her left arm. "How lucky you are to have such robust late summer roses. Mine have all but finished now." He cupped one of them. "'Iceberg'?"

"Yes."

"Beautiful."

"Pity they have so little fragrance," said Elizabeth.

"Oh, there's fragrance there, you know. But it's very subtle."

They walked slowly to the open front door. "I do hope you'll be comfortable."

"I'm sure I will."

"I've some champagne on ice waiting in the lounge," said Elizabeth. "I didn't want you to think us ostentatious, but it is rather refreshing after a long drive. In any case, I wanted to offer you a little toast."

"A toast?"

"To a pleasant stay."

"How charming."

She took his arm and guided him inside the Dower House, knowing that, so far, his impression of Glendarroch was favourable.

It was the first time for several days that Jimmy had come in early for his tea. Isabel looked up from serving a customer and registered a mild surprise. She watched him take a small carton of orange juice from the chiller cabinet and dig into his jeans for the money. The Blairs had a rule—they never took anything from the store without paying for it. She nodded as he put the coins on the counter and finished serving her customer. She and Jimmy bade the woman good day as she left.

Isabel rang up the sale on the till. "Och, you nearly gave me a heart failure, lad," she said, with mock concern. "There's nothing wrong, is there? We've not seen you back this early for ages. Is it snowing down by the lochside, then?"

"It might just as well be," said Jimmy. "Water's icy cold and there are no skiers today."

"No one down there at all?" asked Isabel, offhandedly.

"No. So I sent Robbie and Alistair away."

"No one at all?" Isabel repeated.

"Ma, I just told you." But he knew what she was getting at.

"No wee blonde lassie wi' a 'bonny pouty mouth'?"

"No, she's away."

"Aaah," said Isabel, extravagantly. "So that explains why you're home at this time. May one ask who ditched who?"

Jimmy grinned at his mother. "No. One may not!"

"Never mind, eh?"

"It's not important." Nevertheless, he decided to change the subject. "So where's dad?"

"He's away over to the Minister's fixing a broken curtain runner in the spare bedroom."

"Oh, he'll come back in a right feckle, then," said Jimmy. "He'll have had Mrs Mack chatterin' away at him all the time. Makes him furious."

"It's alright. He can handle it."

"He shouldn't have to, ma. Anyway, fixing a curtain runner's no job for a grown man! Mrs Mack could've done it hersel'."

"Your father has to keep busy, Jimmy. You know that," said Isabel, quietly.

"Doing that sort of work? For Mrs Mack for goodness sake?"

Isabel turned away and straightened some tins up on the nearest shelf. "He's been lucky, you know," she said. "He's kept himself fully occupied these past months—always doing something or other. Odd jobs . . . Och, he's earned a few quid. It all helps."

Jimmy had finished his orange juice and tossed the empty carton into the large waste-basket by the chiller cabinet. "Aye, but that was the summer, ma. You can always keep yoursel' busy when the sun's out. There are odd jobs to do—for the Estate, for folk in the village, for the tourists . . . But there's not much for anyone in the winter, is there? Och, he must know that. It must be worrying him no end," he said, with some depth of feeling. The oncoming winter was worring Jimmy, too, for he knew it was far worse for his father. Brian Blair would feel trapped and useless. The anger, the fury, the 'Blair temper' would torment and frustrate him again. He was under licence, he had a criminal record, so he would be the last to be offered any of the decent work that might become available. So far he had kept everything in check, his personal safety-valve was holding. He would never starve, of course: there was Isabel's income from their shop and Jimmy's accrued profit from the Aqua Sports—but that, somehow, made it worse for Brian. It had the effect of emasculating him, he would be dependant on them and that would deprive him of his manhood. The valve might blow. Soon. Maybe in anticipation. The resulting explosion would be awful. Brian, the kind, good humoured, sensible father figure, would perhaps do something stupid and violent.

Jimmy moved to his mother and instinctively put an arm about her shoulders as she fiddled with the can on the shelf. He could feel her trembling very slightly and knew she was thinking the same thoughts. "We'll be alright," she said, without turning to face him.

"Does he have any work for tomorrow?" Jimmy asked.

"Aye," said Isabel, " a good job tomorrow. A really good one. He has some fencing to do for the Forestry up on Ardvain, not far from the Lachlan place. He'll enjoy that. He loves Ardvain—and the pay is very good . . . Yes, he likes it up there." She knew she was talking about Brian as though he were some invalid, some helpless cretin to be protected. She loathed doing that.

"How many days work, ma?"

"Just two," said Isabel. "But by then it'll be time for me to do the stock-taking here—and I'll need him to help me for that . . ."She turned to Jimmy then—and she could see that he knew exactly when the stock-taking was really due to be done. There was a tremor in her voice as she said: "I hate it when the summer ends, Jimmy."

"Between you and me, Mrs Cunningham," Sir Jeffrey was saying, "the whole concept is quite ludicrous." Elizabeth arched an eyebrow delicately. She decided to show no more reaction than that, until she had absorbed more of the 'concept' he spoke of.

Sawyer had just unobtrusively topped up their glasses for the second time. The champagne was excellent, its temperature exactly right and the view through the french-windows tranquil and soothing. The abundance of huge oaks and beeches screened the more dramatic scenery from them. A panorama of Ben Darroch, the loch and Ardvain would be just a little too breathtaking at this time of the early evening. It would intrude on the conversation, restrict its flow.

Elizabeth had intended to have just one half glass of champagne with Sir Jeffrey—to see him settled in, as it were, and to ensure that the Sawyers could find everything—but that had been an hour ago. Sir Jeffrey had insisted she join him at the french windows to drink just a little more of the Taittinger—and to talk for a while and thereby allow them to become less than total strangers.

"Why is it ludicrous?" asked Elizabeth, carefully.

"A Trade Union Pension Fund—a very worthy, but extremely militant, Left Wing Trade Union at that—with assets of many millions of pounds, subscribed from the wages of its Members," explained Sir Jeffrey, "investing in a completely reactionary enterprise such as Glendarroch Estate? This entire place is a bastion of all they have ever fought against. Your father, Sir Logan Peddie, Laird of Glendarroch, was the enemy. Now, if I recommend it, they will *own* every acre and brick of it." He took a sip of his champagne and looked at Elizabeth over the rim of the glass. "Don't you find that—if not ludicrous, then somewhat ironic?"

"The world has changed," said Elizabeth. "One would be a fool to pretend it hasn't."

"The world has changed. Oh yes. In most other places. But, strangely enough, not all that much on the shop floor of a large factory. Not in the attitude of those who still think in terms of 'them' and 'us'. Many of their representatives would be absolutely shocked, for instance, if they knew that *I* was advising them on their financial investments." He laughed. "The only time I can ever remember wearing a pair of overalls was in the days of my youth when I tinkered with the engine of my father's racing Bentley."

"White overalls?" Elizabeth asked. And her eyes danced with mischief.

"As a matter of fact—yes."

Elizabeth gazed at the busy bubbles in her champagne as they materialised magically at the bottom of the glass from nowhere and then sped to the surface. "I'm afraid you're far more reactionary than anyone here in Glendarroch has ever been," she said. "My father spent most of his working life in old corduroy trousers and patched jackets that your shop floor people wouldn't be seen dead in! Our tenant farmers usually sport overalls that are so stained and work-worn that it is impossible to tell, even on close examination, what colour they started out!"

"So it doesn't worry you that you may end up being owned by a Pension Fund?"

"We should welcome it. Whether they like it or not, at least they are our own kindred, regardless of any barriers they may feel inclined to erect." She regarded him seriously. "I have never liked the idea of foreigners owning Scottish land."

"An understandable—if somewhat parochial—attitude. Emotionally I agree with you."

"But the heart should not rule the bank balance?" suggested Elizabeth.

"In our case," said Sir Jeffrey, "it is even a little more complex than that." He leaned back a little in his chair and turned his gaze from Elizabeth to a far oak standing at the bottom of the Dower garden. It looked like a green-cassocked giant endeavouring to embrace the sky. "We are a Scottish-based organisation, we have vast financial resources, Glendarroch Estate appears to be the sort of long term investment we seek . . ." He stopped.

"But?" prompted Elizabeth.

"But we must not be *seen* to be interested," he said, slowly. "Do you understand? Politically this is an embarrassing investment."

" 'Bastion of all they have ever fought against'?" prompted Elizabeth.

"Exactly." He turned back to her. "I am down here, to all intents and purposes, to enjoy a short vacation, a tiny respite from the arduous duties of the Board Room. No more than that. Fortunately, there is no likelihood of the Press trailing me down here. Which is just as well. Because if certain sections of the Press should get wind of any prospective deal, any interest whatsoever in our possible purchase of the Estate—they would have a field day! I should then have to deny, most emphatically, the whole story." He nodded. "Yes, dear lady, that would be an end to it. I should thank you most courteously for your splendid hospitality, get into my car, immediately drive away—and cross 'Glendarroch Estate' off my confidential agenda. My Board would hear no more proposition." He looked apologetic. "I'm sorry—but that is the way it must be."

"Of course," agreed Elizabeth.

"Whilst I am here there should be no fuss, no bother, no spotlight. That's why I have chosen this time of the year. It is quietening down again after the holiday season. I can look around the Estate—and attract little attention." Sir Jeffrey smiled gently. "And if I was to have you as my guide—that would change a business chore into a profound pleasure."

For the first time in more years than she cared to count, Elizabeth Cunningham felt a blush glow into her cheeks. And she wondered why.

6

High Road to Ardvain

Brian Blair had a bad night. Isabel could feel him writhe, every now and again, as the anger stabbed at him.

Evidently Mrs Mack had been in fine form. She had stood behind Brian as he worked—and the innuendoes, carefully wrapped in syrupy sentiments and misquotes from the Bible, had flown thick and fast. He had come home late, trembling with suppressed fury.

Jimmy wondered if Mrs Mack knew how close she had come to unleashing a storm of violence against her own person. Anyway, he was glad that he was on hand when his father got back. His mother could cope perfectly well, he knew, but it was good that they faced this 'black curse' as Isabel had once labelled it, together, all three of them.

He heard Brian get up from his bed at two in the morning and go into the kitchen. A minute later he heard his mother follow. He listened as she ran the water into the kettle and knew they were going to talk it out over the inevitable cup of tea. She would listen as the snarling words poured out of him, she would hold his shivering hand and dry the sweat of fear from his brow as the vileness escaped. If she was successful he would hear the water again as they washed up the teapot and their two cups. It usually took about half an hour.

But Jimmy was still listening to hear the tap two and a half hours later. He fell asleep at four-thirty, still waiting.

The next morning, when Jimmy came down, he found the two cups by the sink, unwashed. His mother looked hollow-eyed and anxious, but busied herself getting their breakfast and chatted away as though nothing was amiss.

Brian looked ghastly. His face was white and there was a nerve twitching uncontrollably at his temple. His lip was swollen and Jimmy guessed that he had bitten into it deeply in his frustration. It was evident that the vileness had not escaped.

Jimmy was pleased that his father would be working up on Ardvain that morning. He could swing that sledg-hammer at the fence stakes and perhaps dissipate some of his temper.

Even the weather had conspired to match Brian's mood. There was more than a smirring over the landscape. It was a foggy murky-grey mist that covered everything, dampened everything. It was accompanied by a chill that seemed to herald winter more than the advent of autumn. Up on Ardvain, in the folds and hollows, the mist gathered quite thickly so that even the sheep scattered away from it and sought out the clearer ground above.

At Mrs MacPhearson's, just outside the village, Moira Moncrieff was apparently untroubled by the weather. She had had a good night's sleep, with Lilian waking only once—and that was promptly at her feeding time. She was really rather looking forward to her drive to Ardvain, though she had no idea exactly where or how she was going to start her search for Lilian's father. Should she just knock at the front door of the first croft she came to—ask to see the man of the house—and then move on to the next cottage if he wasn't the one? She wasn't all that concerned. She would take her time. She had not even conceived of the possibility that Lilian's father may have left Ardvain—or never have lived there at all. She would, she decided, cross one bridge at a time.

Molly MacPhearson had tried hard to dissuade her from driving into the high country. For anyone who did not know the twists, and turns, that road, Molly knew, could be treacherous, especially in this type of weather. It was a single track and some of the crofters thought they were aspiring Stirling Mosses when they got behind the wheels of their battered Landrovers.

Meanwhile, in the Lachlan croft, up in Ardvain, Grace was doing her darndest to get Dougal *out* of doors to start the day's work. He was secretly delighted to have Donald back under his roof, even if it was only temporary—until Alice could manage again. Dougal was not one to be over demonstrative, nor was he given to skylarking with children—but breakfast this morning had been a sore trial for Grace. Wee Donald was chattering away, most of it in his own 'mixtie-maxtie' nonsense language, but occasionally an identifiable word would come out—and it drew from Dougal a roar of approval and surprise. This would be followed by a dedicated attempt to hold a serious conversation with the boy.

"Now, did you hear that, mother?" exclaimed Dougal. "That was 'Lachlan' the boy said—as plain as could be . . ."

"Rubbish," said Grace. "He was spittin' out his porridge, that's all." She wagged a finger at Donald. "And if he does it again he's going to get a smack from his grannie!"

"It was 'Lachlan', I tell you. It's not an easy word to say, mind—but it was 'Lachlan'."

"Daphnup!" said Donald, and a fresh spray of porridge went over the table.

"You see?" shouted Dougal, excitedly. " 'Lachlan'. Plain as can be! Och, he'll be readin' before you know it!"

"Yer glaikit lumph," said Grace, disdainfully. "Can you read now?"

"Of course I can . . ."

"Then read what that clock says, Dougal! Just look at the time. You should've been off and about your work nearly an hour ago!"

"Aye, I'm going, I'm going!" And Dougal moved reluctantly towards the door. "Will you be alright, then? On your own?"

"Och, of course I will. Away with you now—and leave me in peace to get on with what I have to do here."

"It was 'Lachlan' he said."

"Chalack!" said Donald.

"You see?" Dougal shouted triumphantly.

"Away!" ordered Grace.

"Aye, but I'll be back for my morning tea . . ."

"It'll be time for it before you get out of that door! Go on, Dougal!"

And he went out. Grace watched the door for a little while, half expecting him to find some excuse to come back in. But she heard him calling for his dog and that meant this day had truly started.

Grace chuckled and poured herself another cup of tea. "Och, you poor wee bairn," she said to Donald, "you've an awfu' daftie for a father, haven't you?" She sighed contentedly. "Well, at least we can relax for a few minutes before I clear away yon breakfast mess, eh?"

"Bleepblah!" said Donald, laughing.

"Sounds nothing like 'Lachlan'," she muttered. "That's 'Grannie' as clear as the tinkle of a bell." And she believed it, too.

The road that leads from the village to Ardvain, the only road up to the Estate-owned crofts, starts out with every good intention. For the first two and a half miles it is wide enough for two vehicles to pass carefully and, though it has never seen tar macadam, it has had gravel laid over it—now and again. But only for the first two and half miles. Thereafter it deteriorates as successive Councils have lost interest in it. It shrinks to a narrow twisting track that gets steeper and bumpier with every mile. There are channels cut by flood waters running alongside it most of the way and ditches worn across it when those same flood waters overflow. It is a mud-slide in the rain and a rutted dust-shute when it's dry. In the snow it is impassable. The Estate has tried to maintain it, but has always fought a losing battle with the elements and the terrain. It keeps an old bulldozer and an even older snow-plough in a shed alongside Mrs MacPhearson's property—but it is always a nerve-racking and dangerous job operating them in the bad weather. Its rough condition keeps the road lonely. Few tourists bother to travel more than the first two and a half miles along it.

It is a further three miles on before you reach the turnoff that takes you out to the lowest of the upland crofts, Robbie Moncur's place. Even he is cut off from the village when the snow begins to lay and drift. Then there is Hamish McNeil's cottage, but that is set well back from the road and nestles behind a shallow fold on a hillside. After that there is a long stretch before you reach the Stewart, Lachlan and the Tulloch crofts. None of them stand at the roadside. For some inexplicable reason all of them have long, winding tracks leading to them, as though they wanted to hide themselves away from the eyes of any infrequent stranger who might, by accident, journey along that road. It was probably, in days gone by, to keep themselves inconspicuous from the likes of the English redcoated soldiers or raiding Clansmen—or inquisitive Taxmen.

And on a day like this, when there was a rolling foggy-mist, grey and opaque, moving sluggishly down the hillsides, you could travel almost to Inveraray—and still miss the crofts, even the most westerly of them, the McNair home. You could be forgiven for believing that this thin, tortuous road merely weaved its way through an uninhabited majestic wilderness.

"Frankfurt's the only problem," Dunbar was saying. They were having an early morning conference in his office, he and Elizabeth, with Lorna Seton taking any notes they might need. They were like conspirators. Only they knew the real reason for Sir Jeffrey Leighton-Fyffe's presence in Glendarroch. Elizabeth had not even mentioned it to Fiona—nor would she. As far as everyone else was concerned, Sir Jeffrey was taking a late holiday. That's all. "If any of Meier's people get an inkling that he's here— they'll start putting two and two together."

"Alright, let them," said Elizabeth. "It doesn't really matter. If they think there's an offer in the wind—then it's to their advantage to keep quiet about it. They wouldn't want it to become public knowledge. They would know it might scare him off. No, I don't think it's Frankfurt we have to worry about." She frowned, exploring in her mind the danger areas. "No, the problem is much more likely to stem from here—from the village. Rumour, speculation, gossip. Someone gets it in their head that Sir Jeffrey is perhaps interested in the Estate, perhaps he's a buyer—some-one like Mrs Mack, for instance—and the word will spread like wildfire. The gutter-press will sniff it out—and our knight in shining armour will be away and back to Glasgow before you can blink an eye. That's how critical it is."

"You can't stop speculation and you can't stop rumours —not in Glendarroch," said Dunbar. "We just have to hope they don't hit on the truth."

"There's too much at stake. Somehow we must find some insurance," Elizabeth pondered.

Lorna looked uncomfortable. Dunbar saw her expression as she sought to hide it. "Something the matter, Lorna?" he asked. "Well . . ." Lorna started.

"We are listening to all ideas and suggestions, Lorna," smiled Elizabeth.

Lorna hesitated for a second. She was a most competent secretary, but she was shy and somewhat introverted. Dunbar and Elizabeth knew that Lorna would never interrupt unless she had something of practical value to offer. They waited.

"There *will* be speculation and rumours, Mrs Cunningham. The Factor is quite right, you can't stop them," Lorna said. "And Sir Jeffrey is obviously quite a 'striking' sort of person—and there is that Rolls-Royce—and his servants . . . It's also late in the season now and there are hardly any other strangers about the area . . . He *will* attract attention." Lorna took a deep breath and consulted her notebook. "I was checking through the proposed itinerary we were planning for Sir Jeffrey . . ." And she quoted from it: "Today—'Lunch at Glendarroch House—with Mrs Cunningham.' This afternoon—'2.30 pm—motor to Ben Darroch and view grouse driving moors—with Mrs Cunningham. Dinner this evening at the Dower House—with Mrs Cunningham. Tomorrow—suggested trip to Ardvain . . .'"

". . . with Mrs Cunningham," added Dunbar.

"Yes."

"Go on, Lorna ," prompted Elizabeth.

"I-I'm sorry, this is a little embarrassing . . . "stuttered Lorna.

"You're doing very well," smiled Dunbar. "Keep going."

"Well, it seems to me," said Lorna, "that we are already sowing the seeds of gossip and speculation." She took another deep breath and kept her attention away from Elizabeth. "It could look as though there was some sort of 'attachment'—er—'liason', perhaps—between Sir Jeffrey and Mrs Cunningham."

"Ah!" said Dunbar.

And once again Elizabeth could feel a suspicion of colour mounting into her cheeks.

"If Sir Jeffrey is here as Mrs Cunningham's *personal* guest," continued Lorna, "the gossip would start and the rumours would fly thick and fast."

"A blossoming romantic attachment?" suggested Dunbar, smiling just a little more broadly now.

That's what most people would think, I'm afraid, Mrs Cunningham," said Lorna.

"Yes, I suppose so," said Elizabeth, drily.

"But it would definitely submerge any other speculation as to why he is here," said Dunbar, enthusiastically. "To outward appearances he has come to Glendarroch to spend a little time relaxing with a most charming lady."

"Thank you," Elizabeth said, very coolly.

"It could work."

Elizabeth regarded Dunbar stonily. "I don't like that sort of subterfuge, Factor," she said. "And I'm sure Sir Jeffrey wouldn't approve, either."

"I'm sure he would," said Dunbar.

"If it was a means to an end," added Lorna, hastily. "One could treat it as a sort of—'cover' plan." She looked down at her notes again, unable to meet Elizabeth's eye. "A sort of insurance. A protection policy. I mean, all you have to do is to be seen together. It's already in the itinerary. It's almost as though it has been pre-planned that way."

Moira quite enjoyed the first two and a half miles of her journey up the Ardvain road, despite the murky weather . The car seemed to be going surprisingly well, though the ruts and potholes were causing her a little trouble. In the back Lilian was lulled by the vibrations and, after a short bout of crying, fell fast asleep.

Moira was fascinated by the view ahead. The first foothills rose from small lakes of fog and mist like islands from an Arthurian legend, as a Victorian Pre-Raphaelite artist might have envisaged them. She half expected to see the stately towers of Camelot rising from the gloom maybe round the next bend. Or a richly canopied barge ferrying a garlanded lady across the grey, hazy insubstantial surface of the mist.

Then the road got bad and she had to concentrate hard on the surface just ahead and cut down her speed drastically. Each bend seemed tighter than the last and the terrain got steeper. Alongside her the foothills turned into looming crags and, in some places, near-vertical banks. Then the little car would dip into a hollow and suddenly become submerged in a spume of damp fog.

It was, therefore, little wonder that, after nearly six miles, she missed the turn-off that led to Robbie Moncur's croft.

She also missed the track to Hamish McNeil's place. Though, as it happened, Hamish saw her, quite clearly, from a bluff that fronted the road. He saw the carry-cot on the rear seat, too. He waved frantically and called loudly to Moira—but she couldn't hear him over the raucous din the little engine made as it strained against the rough incline. He scrambled down from the bluff amidst a skelter of tiny pebbles and rocks to chase after the Mini—but there was another dip in the road and the car gathered speed. He ran for a few yards—then gave up after a while and decided he would look out for her on her way back. Hamish did not know she had missed the way to Moncur's as well.

So Moira drove on and lost all account of time and distance. In the back of her mind was the nagging belief that she should have seen some signs of habitation before this—but she could not be sure how far she had travelled.

Lilian, who had slept blissfully through the twists and bumps of the journey until then, woke suddenly and began to cry loudly—those great wailing sobs that would not abate until Moira took her in her arms. However, at that very moment Moira steered into a very tight bend . . .

. . . And drove straight into a dense blanket of thick fog that lay across the road like a grey-green barrier. The thickest yet: blinding her completely. She pumped at the brake, locking the Mini's wheels, causing it to slither round uncontrollably, spinning it and drawing it to the unseen dangers on either side.

It was then that she began to scream, adding her own terror-filled voice to the cries of her daughter—filling the inside of the little car with an awsome cacophony of sound.

7

A Growl of Thunder

Dougal had decided that this was going to be one of those years when they would have no autumn at all. They would go straight from the temperate ease of summer into the lashing storms and blizzards of winter. At least, up here in Ardvain they would. In the meantime they would have a couple of days like today, which were neither one thing nor the other. Strange, limbo days—not summer, autumn or winter. Too warm for his Arran jersey and anorak, too cold for a thin windcheater. So he was wearing an old jacket—and he hated working in a jacket.

There were still pockets of fog clinging to the hollows and he would have to check those down by the road to make sure that none of his sheep had strayed away from the main flocks on the upper slopes. There were peaty bogs down there, too, and some of the younger beasts would be stuck.

He noticed the sky was darkening over and guessed there would be a storm before long. At least it might clear the fog pockets and the ground-clinging shreds of mist that were making walking difficult. In some places it was like stepping through puddles of cold steam.

He was moving downhill and his bitch, Tav, always nervous when the weather was 'heavy', was darting about excitedly. He still had to watch her carefully, not like his old dog, Laddie, who loped like a silent shadow through the gorse and heather, covering twice as much ground. An instruction to Laddie never had to be repeated, with Tav he always had to call two or three times.

As he reached the road he heard a Landrover approaching. On Ardvain the crofters could identify each others' vehicles by the tone of their engines, each like a distinctive signature tune (Tulloch's had a crack in the silencer and it gave out with a deep-throated roar that could be heard a mile and a half away, Jamie Lockhart drove one of those Japanese jeep-type things that had a whiney sound to it, Tam Shaw belted his Landrover so hard that its engine sounded as though it was complaining all the time . . .). The Landrover he heard now, even though he could not see it yet because there were a couple of bends between it and him, belonged to Morag Stewart. She drove well and she did a good job of servicing the machine herself, but it was old and cantankerous—it growled bad-temperedly as it negotiated each turn in the steep road. Morag would be on her way to spend the morning with Grace and Donald at the Lachlan croft. It was good of her to forsake her own work about her croft like that, thought Dougal. Dr Wallace would have seen her yesterday to talk about Alice and Morag would not have hesitated to volunteer to help.

Then he heard the Landrover come to a halt some distance away, its engine still idling. Morag had stopped for some reason. Maybe a dead or crippled sheep on the road—and it would be one of Dougal's no doubt. He swore under his breath, then called to Tav and began running down along the road towards the sound.

As he came round the second bend he saw that it wasn't any crippled beast on the road. Morag had stopped next to a small, dull blue little Mini whose nose was buried in the deep ditch that ran along the inside edge of the tight turn. It was tilted at such a steep angle that its rear wheels were clear of the road. The windscreen was shattered, a whole wing was buckled, and both doors were yawning open. Through one of them Morag was dragging the body of Moira Moncrieff from behind the wheel.

"Oh, my God!" Dougal exclaimed, as he hurried to help her. Ironically, the lethal bank of fog had drifted away and the bend was clear.

"It's Moira," gasped Morag, as Dougal joined her. "She's alive!" Together they lifted her clear and Dougal carried her to the side, whilst Morag returned quickly to the Mini. She pushed forward the passenger seat and began searching in the back.

"Morag," shouted Dougal, "I need something for her head . . ."

But Morag ignored him. Dougal laid Moira down carefully and took off his jacket to make a pillow for her. There was a nasty gash on her temple, obviously where she had hit her head on the steering wheel, but there was very little blood. Fortunately, Dougal was a member of the local Mountain Rescue Team and he knew the rudiments of First Aid. He was glad to see there was no blood coming from Moira's ears, mouth or nose, though she looked deathly pale. It was concussion, but it was impossible to say how bad. Her breathing was shallow and her pulse racing.

Morag was calling him: "Dougal, come here, quickly!"

"Listen, I can't leave her—and we need to keep her warm!"

"Come here!" Morag shouted, urgently. There was desperation in her voice. Dougal rose and ran quickly over to the Mini.

"Moira's unconscious . . ." began Dougal.

"*There should be a baby in here, Dougal!*" said Morag, turning to him, her eyes wide with alarm.

"What?"

"She was travelling with her baby. There's its carrycot in the back—here—pillow, mattress and everything . . . But there's no sign of the wean!"

Dougal pushed Morag aside. "Cover Moira," he said. "Keep her warm." Morag hesitated. "Go on now," he insisted. She hurried away to the unconscious girl.

Dougal searched the inside of the Mini carefully. Miraculously the carry-cot had remained safely jammed on the back seat. Judging by the relatively small amount of damage, the impact had not been all that great. Certainly not enough to fling the baby from the back past the mother and through the shattered windscreen. Anyway, there was no sign of the child outside. He searched inside the cot itself. Moira's handbag was at the foot of it. He opened it and found it was crammed with money. He snapped it shut again hurriedly and replaced the bag exactly where he found it.

Then he looked quickly, but thoroughly, all around the outside of the car. Even under it. There was no sign of any baby.

Morag, meanwhile, had taken a blanket from her Land-rover and covered Moira. She had switched on the head and rear lights to warn any approaching vehicle of the danger.

Dougal rejoined her. Morag looked up at him anxiously. It's the blanket we use to wrap the weaklings in at lambing time. It's no' awfy clean . . ."

"There's no baby there, Morag," said Dougal. "Are you sure there was one in the car to start with?"

"Och, did you not see the carry-cot, Dougal?"

"Maybe she left the wean down in Glendarroch . . ."

"You can tell there was a baby in that cot!" insisted Morag, her voice rising.

"What happened, then?"

"What do you mean—'what happened'? It was like that when I drove up! Exactly like that, man! You saw me getting Moira out, didn't you?" She became suddenly angry. "Look, you don't think I pushed her off the road *just now*, do you?" she asked, indignantly. "My God, you would've heard . . ."

"Och, no, Morag, don't be daft. I felt the bonnet. The engine's stone cold. She's been stuck here for more than an hour and a half, that's for sure!" He stared at the car. "No, I mean, was it like that when you first saw it? Doors open, an a'?" said Dougal.

"Aye."

He shook his head slowly. "Doors open?" he repeated, hushed.

"Come on, Dougal, let's get this poor woman up to your mother's place . . ." said Morag. "Or do you think she shouldna be moved? Might be something broken inside, eh?"

"No, I don't think so," said Dougal. "Anyway, we can't leave her lying here whilst we wait for the ambulance from Auchtarne. We'll lift her carefully into the back of your Landrover and we'll take her up to my place. Then I'll drive down to the phone box past Moncur's and call Dr Wallace, whilst you and my mother tend to her."

"Alright, then," agreed Morag. She knelt down and felt Moira's brow. "Och, she's icy cold, Dougal." She tucked the blanket round Moira's shoulders as Dougal bent to get his arms under the unconscious woman's body. Morag prepared to help him take some of the weight. "Poor thing," she said.

"I'd like to know what happened," said Dougal.

"I'd like to know what's happened to her wee baby!" said Morag.

They lifted Moira Moncrieff gently and carried her to the Landrover.

At Glendarroch House, in Elizabeth's flat, there were files
and documents strewn over every inch of her large dining
table. For two hours she and Dunbar had explained,
analysed, discussed and tabulated every fact and figure
about the Estate they thought relevant. Naturally, they had
to condense a lot, but they did not, purposely, paint an
over-rosy picture of the situation or the potential of the
place as an investment. They were honest, Elizabeth had
insisted that they should be, and they were realistic. Sir
Jeffrey appreciated that and he listened quietly and
intently, interrupting only once in a while to get clarifica-
tion of some detail. Of course, there were certain aspects
of the Company structure that they could not discuss and
Sir Jeffrey did not press for any information that might be
construed as confidential. He was astute enough to draw
his own conclusions about those areas left unexplored.

As the Regency mantle clock over the fireplace
delicately chimed twelve noon, Sir Jeffrey raised his hand,
smiled and adjourned the proceedings.

It was difficult for the Factor or Elizabeth to know what sort
of impression they had made on him. His smile was totally
enigmatic and it gave nothing away. Elizabeth suggested
sherries—and it was only then that the smile warmed to a
genuine expression of pleasure. They drank an extremely rare
Palo Cortado, a vintage Oloroso, one of the few valuable wines
Elizabeth had managed to salvage and hide away from the
Frankfurt buyers. They had swarmed through Glendarroch
House cellars like locusts, shipping everything they could lay
their hands on back to their summer chalets on the slopes of
the Taunus Mountains above the River Main: wines that had
taken Sir Logan Peddie, and his father before him, dedicated
lifetimes apiece to collect.

Afterwards Dunbar gathered up all the papers and
documents and took his leave, knowing that Elizabeth and
Sir Jeffrey were having luncheon together. Instinctively he
knew that his own prolonged presence would hinder
rather than help things along, even though Elizabeth had
said there was sufficient Chicken Galantine for them all. It
was, at best, he knew, a half-hearted invitation, offered—
specifically to be declined.

"Chicken Galantine?" said Sir Jeffrey, after Dunbar had
gone.

"With a walnut salad," added Elizabeth. "I do hope you approve."

"Positively. Providing you're serving it with a chablis rather than a German wine." He allowed that smile to dwindle a little.

She knew he was gently teasing her. "A very unenterprising little chablis, I'm afraid. But then I'm not too fond of German wines."

"No real delicacy," he said. "No *finesse*."

"What time would you like to eat? There's nothing to cook. I can serve it whenever you like."

"It's a little early yet, isn't it? Perhaps we could go for a little stroll first," he suggested.

"Well, I'm afraid the gardens aren't what they used to be. . ."

"No, I was thinking that a little walk through the village might be rather nice." He put his empty sherry glass down on the table beside him. "Or would it be too boring for you, do you think, Elizabeth?"

"Not at all." And now it was her turn to smile. She realised that he knew there was a game to play. Sir Jeffrey fully understood the little subterfuge and had even anticipated Lorna Seton's 'cover plan'.

Moira Moncreiff had still not regained consciousness when Dougal left the croft and drove as fast as he could down to the phone box below Moncur's place.

Morag and Grace had put the girl to bed, placed hot water bottles at her feet and a good eider quilt over her. Until the arrival of Dr Wallace, there was no more they could do but sit and watch over her. Morag explained who she was—and what she was doing up in Ardvain. She also told Grace about the missing baby.

When Dougal got to the phone box he made two calls. The first to Dr Wallace's Surgery to tell his Receptionist abut Moira. The lass said she knew where she could contact Dr Wallace and would send him straight up.

The other call he made was to Mrs MacPhearson. Morag had already told him that Moira was probably staying there on Isabel Blair's recommendation. He asked Molly if Moira had been carrying her baby in the little car when she left that morning. Molly confirmed his fears and, naturally, she wanted to know what had happened.

After they had finished speaking, it was Molly Mac-Phearson who rang through to the Police in Auchtarne to report the whole matter.

Elizabeth and Sir Jeffrey strolled along the main street of the village, slowly past Blair's Store and down to the tiny jetty that stuck out into the loch. They were both wearing raincoats because the air was heavy with moisture and there was an ominous rumble or two of thunder from the other side of Ardvain. However, they talked animatedly and refused to allow the deteriorating weather to put a damper on their obvious interest in each other.

Mrs Mack was watching them through the Blair shop window, peering at them, desperately trying to interpret their every gesture. Isabel and Lorna, back at the counter, were watching her. It was a shame, Lorna thought, that Murdoch was not in the store just now. She would have loved to hear the speculative duologue that would have gone on between them. Even so, Mrs Mack was trying to ferret out every ounce of information she could. She assumed, in this case, that Lorna would at least know something.

"Come on, Lorna," said Mrs Mack, "you must know who he is. Och, he was away up to the House this morning in the biggest motorcar you ever saw! All gleaming and polished. Mr Murdoch said it was a Rolls-Royce, a new one. And there are not too many people who can afford new Rolls-Royces these days, eh? Just look at his clothes, will you? That raincoat must've come from London."

"More likely Jenners in Edinburgh," said Isabel.

"It would've cost a pretty penny, anyway," said Mrs Mack, her eyes still glued to Elizabeth and Sir Jeffrey through the window. Who is he, Lorna?"

"Oh, I don't know, Mrs Mack," Lorna lied. "Just a friend of Mrs Cunningham's that's all."

"She is allowed to have friends, you know," Isabel added.

"He's someone important, I'd say," insisted Mrs Mack.

Lorna shrugged. "Maybe to her—yes."

And now Isabel turned her attention from Mrs Mack and looked at Lorna. "Oh?" she said.

"Aye," answered Lorna. "But I don't know, for certain."

Alice Taylor, played by Muriel Romanes, gives Wee Donald (Stuart Herd) a helping hand. Elizabeth Cunningham (Edith Macarthur) looks on encouragingly.

Loch Darroch and the slopes of Ben Darroch form the background to this informal portrait of some of the "Take The High Road" cast. The whitewashed walls of the Glendarroch Store can be seen on the left.

Alec Monteath (left) plays Dougal Lachlan, crofter and shepherd. Here he shows Hamish McNeil (William Armour) over the Estate.

"Just good friends". Caroline Ashley plays the part of Fiona Cunningham, seen here with Jimmy Blair, played by Jimmy Chisholm.

Marjorie Thomson as Grace Lachlan enjoys a reassuring hug from Bob Taylor, played by Iain Agnew.

Edith Macarthur as the "Lady Laird", Elizabeth Cunningham.

Farmer Alex Geddes played by James Cosmo in conversation with Fiona Cunningham (Caroline Ashley).

Bob and Alice's wedding, from a previous series. Left to right: Grace Lachlan (Marjorie Thomson), the factor Douglas Dunbar (Clive Graham) as Best Man, Bridegroom Bob Taylor (Iain Agnew), the Bride Alice (Muriel Romanes), the Bridesmaid Morag Stewart (Jeannie Fisher) and Dougal Lachlan (Alec Monteath), who gave the bride away.

The day the Wedding Episode was filmed was certainly "wellies weather", as Director Hal Duncan fully appreciated!

Filming a scene outside the Taylor's cottage, including Dougal Lachlan, Alice Taylor, Wee Donald and Grace Lachlan, with one of the Glendarroch Estate Land Rovers.

Bill Henderson as Ken Calder, a mechanic at Duff's Garage, prepares to load the van. Here he receives instructions from Director Paul Kimberly, with Camera Sound ready for action.

Eileen McCallum
as Isabel Blair, the
shopkeeper of the
Glendarroch Store.

Clive Graham as
Douglas Dunbar,
the Factor.

Jim Byars as
Graeme B. Hogg

Joan Alcorn as
Lorna Seton

Paul Kermack as
Archie Menzies.

The entire "Take The High Road" cast and crew on the Glendarroch Store set in Scottish Television's Studios, Edinburgh, with Don Houghton, author and first script-editor of the series, standing front row centre.

"You wouldn't've said, then," said Mrs Mack.

"Does it matter? After all, it's Mrs Cunningham's business, isn't it?" said Lorna, wondering if she had gone just a little too far.

Isabel smiled wistfully. "Nice if Mrs Cunningham found herself a beau."

"At her age?" exclaimed Mrs Mack. "Now you know I don't like criticising anyone—least of all our good Lady Laird—but it's just not seemly for anyone of her 'seniority' to be seen flirting in public with a mature gentleman. . ."

"She's not flirting!" Lorna interrupted indignantly. "She happens to be taking a pre-luncheon stroll down the main street of our village with a gentleman, that's all!"

"And," added Isabel, "Mrs Cunningham *is* divorced, single and fancy-free. She is quite entitled to have gentleman friends—mature—or adolescent, come to that!"

Mrs Mack dragged her eyes away from the window and confronted Isabel and Lorna. "She has a position to maintain here," she said, sternly. "She has to be very careful how she conducts herself. There are those who look to her to set an example. I mean, if you can't count on the old Laird's only daughter for moral guidance—who can you count on? She has a duty to the community."

Lorna was getting angry now. "She is not doing anything wrong!"

Mrs Mack sniffed. "Well, we don't know about that, do we? As the Good Book says: 'If we say we have no sin, we are telling lies and are deceiving all. . .' " she misquoted.

Isabel corrected her. " 'If we say we have no sin, we deceive ourselves, and the truth is not in us': is what the Good Book says."

"Aye, well, of course you're quoting from the old King James Version. . . " Mrs Mack countered, unconvincingly. "Anyway, that's not the point. It's just that we don't want temptation put in her path. . ."

"Speak for yourself," said Isabel, grinning broadly. "Maybe Elizabeth Cunningham wouldn't mind a wee bit of temptation across her path once in a while, eh, Lorna?" She turned to Lorna and winked. "It must be lonely for her all alone in that big House."

"Aye," said Lorna, "lonely. . ."

"There's a lot of us know what lonely is," said Mrs Mack

dolefully. "Me especially. I've had to suffer loneliness ever since Mr Mack passed on. . . But I've borne it with no complaint all these years. It just takes a little will power and discipline, that's all."

"And a certain lack of opportunity," added Isabel, quietly.

Mrs Mack gave her an icy look and turned back to the window. She peered forward suddenly. "They've gone!" she yelped.

"And why not?" asked Lorna. "It's nearly lunch time."

"Thank goodness," sighed Isabel, almost under her breath.

Mrs Mack came away from the window reluctantly and joined Lorna at the counter. "Must be in the blood, eh?"

"What?" asked Isabel.

"The need for them to sin." She nodded towards the window. "The Peddies."

"I don't understand," said Isabel.

"The old Laird was no better than he should be, was he?"

"Och, you do talk a lot of rubbish sometimes. . ." began Isabel.

"Then there's Miss Fiona and that uncouth tenant farmer, Geddes. And now Mrs Cunningham herself. . . Aye," sighed Mrs Mack, "it was the curse of a lot of those aristocrats, you know. Bad blood. It led to wicked ways. It'll show in generations to come, mark my words." She collected the tin of sardines and the small packet of rye biscuits from the counter top—they should consitute the bulk of the Minister's meal that night—and gave Isabel and Lorna a pair of sad, baleful smiles. "It's always so nice talking to good friends, isn't it?" She moved to the shop door, whilst neither Lorna nor Isabel trusted themselves to say a word. Mrs Mack stopped just a step or two from it and turned for her parting shot. She smiled directly at Lorna and said, with no warmth in her voice at all: "How's Ken Calder these days, Lorna? Still sharing your roof, is he?"

As Mrs Mack opened the door and went out there was the distant, unaccustomed sound of a police siren. And that was followed by a low, tympanic growl of thunder as the threatened storm approached Ardvain.

8

Cloudburst

Dougal called on Robbie Moncur and Hamish McNeil after he had used the phone box. Hamish told him he had seen Moira's car and had been close enough to notice the cot on the back seat. That had been about nine-thirty and he remembered the pockets of fog had been pretty thick then. She could easily have missed the turning to the Moncur and McNeil crofts. Hamish insisted that he had tried to attract Moira's attention, but she could not have seen him. He thought, at the time, the little Mini would have trouble negotiating the twists and inclines farther up.

Anyway, Hamish and Robbie would immediately spread the word over Ardvain and the crofters would stand-by to offer whatever help the police might need. The mystery of the missing baby was tragically baffling to them. They were sure there had been hardly any traffic on the road. Earlier on, Robbie said, round about eight-thirty, a Forestry vehicle had been by, but that's all he knew about it. He had been working away from the road after that.

Dougal drove on up to his own place, stopping only by the crashed Mini to have a last look around. Perhaps in their anxiety to get Moira up to the croft they had missed something. He checked the verges on either side. He was an experienced deer-stalker and could read the ground for signs, but in this instance it told him nothing.

Moira Moncrieff was still unconscious when he got back to his croft.

Molly MacPhearson was not a Glendarroch gossip, but Dougal's phone call had upset her a great deal. And when she was upset she felt the need to talk to someone. Isabel was, inevitably, her first choice. Jeannie Roxburgh had called her a bit of a dragon and even Isabel had warned Moira that Molly had a reputation for being something of a battleaxe. In fact, nothing could have been farther from the truth. Her brusqueness was Molly's thin shield against an inclement world and an unending file of over-demanding guests. The latter (with, to be fair, some exceptions) now crawled all over the home she and Stan MacPhearson had so lovingly furnished together. She was terse with them, on occasions, to hide the hurt indignation she felt in having strangers share her home and her table. Nevertheless, under it all she was a kind, thoughtful soul, who had not taken easily to widowhood. She suffered, quite often, from the Glendarroch disease—loneliness.

It was nearly five-to-one when she got to Blair's Store. Only Murdoch was there and he moved away from the counter as Molly came in. He went to have a browse through the magazine-racks, as usual, certain that Molly wanted to talk to Isabel—judging by the taut expression on the widow-woman's face. He was a man who could blend into the background and almost disappear from view. However, he would remain just within earshot. Molly MacPhearson's guest house was often a rich source of gossip. Maybe he could pick up a little tid-bit to pass on to the formidable Mrs Mack.

Ignoring Murdoch completely, Molly told Isabel about Moira's car crash—and the missing baby. In some way she felt personally responsible for it, she said. "I warned her about that Ardvain road, Isabel," she insisted. "I told her it was a disgrace. . . Och, but she was a very self-willed lass. There was something or someone she had to see up there." Molly's eyes grew moist. "Oh, and if you had seen that bonny, wee baby. . . And now what's happened to the poor mite, eh?" she said. "She could've left it wi' me. She could've gone up that blasted road on her own and left the wean mi' me. It'd've been safe wi' me, Isabel."

"Did you know who she was?"

"No," said Molly. "Only that she was from Lanark and she came to me on your recommendation. That was enough."

"She was a barmaid at a pub near Lanark Market. Morag Stewart recognised her."

Molly was too distraught to see the immediate significance of that. "I don't care who she was. She was a nice woman, she had good manners and she looked after that baby well. It was clean and healthy. She cared," said Molly.

Murdoch was glancing through the pages of a diet magazine—and seeing nothing. But he had heard every word of Molly's agitated conversation with Isabel. Heard quite clearly. No, he decided, this was not a tid-bit for Mrs

Mack. This was a bigger proposition and there was a few pounds to be made here.

Murdoch knew that Arthur Chisholm, a reporter for the *Auchtarne Gazette* often paid as much as a fiver for the lead on an interesting story. Murdoch reckoned this could be worth ten pounds— a car crash, woman unconscious, missing baby—there was a lot of interest in it. Yes, he'd ask for ten pounds to start with. But he would settle for seven pounds, fifty—if he had to.

He was impatient, now, for them to finish talking so that he could leave without missing anything and without drawing attention to himself. He wanted to get to the phone box down by the jetty. He wondered if Chisholm went out for his mid-day meal—or did he take sandwiches in his office?

Dr Wallace and the police arrived at the Lachlan croft within five minutes of each other. Grace took Wallace straight in to see Moira and stayed with him whilst he made his examination. Moira remained unconscious throughout.

When the police came Dougal and Morag told Sergeant Murray all they knew about Moira Moncrieff—and finding the car—whilst his Constable was sent back to examine the Mini and stand watch over it.

Black clouds were now spreading thickly over Ardvain and the sound of the thunder was drawing closer. There were flashes of distant lightning beyond Beinn Drimfern and the crofters knew that those heavy clouds above them would spill out a lot of driving rain. The burns, rivulets, storm-channels and ditches would be full of rushing water before the day was out.

"Looks to me as though she drove into a patch of fog that was hiding the bend from her," said Sergeant Murray. "She panicked, put her foot too hard on the brake—and skidded into the side."

Dougal looked doubtful. "Maybe," he said, with little conviction.

"Well, what do you think happened, Dougal?" asked the Sergeant.

"She couldna' been travelling all that fast—and she must've driven through a dozen other pockets of fog before she got to that one. Aye, she might've skidded a wee bit—a foot or two, say—but not enough to send her into that ditch. She couldna' turned broadside onto the road—but it seemed to me that car was *driven* into yon ditch."

"By her? 'Cos Morag found her still behind the wheel, mind?"

"I don't know. Och, you're the policeman, Iain Murray—no' me!" said Dougal, impatiently. "But she went into that ditch hard enough to shatter the windscreen!"

"And with enough impact to fling open both the car doors," added Morag.

"No," said Dougal, emphatically. "It wasna' the force of the impact that opened the doors—otherwise the bonnet would've been stove in a lot more than it was. Aye, and Moira would be sufferin' from more than a bang on her head! She'd've smashed in her skull, for certain!"

"Then how did the doors come to be open?" asked the Sergeant.

"You turn the handles—and you pull," said Dougal with heavy sarcasm.

"You mean, someone was there before me?" Morag asked, surprised.

"I don't know," muttered Dougal—and he pointed to the Sergeant. "Ask him, he's the policeman."

The Sergeant didn't take umbrage. He and Dougal were old friends and he had a lot of respect for the crofter. He knew, full well, that there was a lot more to Dougal than folk gave him credit for—and up here Dougal was the expert. He would have a useful instinct that would not be found in any Police Manual. "So someone came along, took the baby—but left the injured mother?"

"I've told you, I don't know," said Dougal. There was something nagging at him. He just could not pinpoint it—and it was making him angry.

"Well, then surely they would have reported it," said Morag. "They'll have taken the baby to one of the crofts—and are away now reporting the accident. . ."

"Which croft?" asked Dougal. "Ours is the nearest. Then there's yours up the road a piece. . .

"And Bob Taylor's cottage down below," said the Sergeant.

It was then that Dougal knew what was bothering him—
what had been bothering him from the moment he had
lifted Moira Moncrieff from out of that little car. He
knew—and suddenly his anger turned to fear and appre-
hension.

The newspapers were not destined to get the story of the
missing baby until much later in the day. Arthur Chisholm
was covering a wedding over on the other side of the loch:
the wedding of an eighty-year-old ghillie to Lord Glengowrie's thirty-year-old stable-maid. His Lordship, full of
admiration for the stamina of the ancient ghillie, had
hosted the Reception after the nuptials. The wine flowed
freely and Arthur Chisholm was working his way steadily
towards a most glorious state of inebriation.

It was, therefore, Murdoch's greed that gave Ardvain a
few precious hours breathing space. He would not give his
story to anyone else at the *Gazette* for fear they would not
pay him for it.

Dr Wallace was washing his hands at the kitchen sink. He
had finished his examination of Moira, which had been
long and thorough, and now he was making his report to
Sergeant Murray. "She's still unconscious," he was saying,
"but maybe that's a Godsend for the moment—in view of
the fact that her wee baby is missing. The shock of that—
on top of the accident. . ." And he shook his head.
"Anyway, I can find no evidence of any fracture, but of
course, I need to have X-Rays as soon as possible, though I
don't want her moved till she's regained consciousness.
And I don't like the idea of a journey down that road just
now. Mrs Lachlan is sitting with her and says she can stay
here for as long as necessary. Her condition seems stable
enough for the time being. Pulse is fairly strong, respiration has picked up a wee bit." He turned off the tap and
Morag handed him a clean towel from the dresser drawer.
"Does the radio in your car reach to Auchtarne from here,
Sergeant?"

"Sometimes," said the Sergeant, "when the conditions
are right. But there's a storm brewing and the airwaves are
full of static. . . My Constable had trouble raising the
Station just before he went back down to the road. You'll
be wanting to get an ambulance up here, Doctor?"

"We'll have to have one—sooner or later."

"Aye, well, we'll get onto that right away. Dougal tells me there'll be some of the crofters up here directly—we can send one of them down to the phone box with the Constable," said the Sergeant. "We'll be starting a search, you see."

"Yes," said Wallace, quietly, "for the baby." And the Doctor purposely kept his attention away from Dougal, so that their eyes would not meet.

The Sergeant frowned. "I have to ask you, Doctor," he said, with difficulty, "how long do you think that wee baby can last out there—without its mother?" He heard Morag take a deep breath.

"It depends," said Wallace, evenly. "It depends where she is—and who she is with. The baby is about three months old, we estimate. It is certainly still being breast fed. . . Even so, they're fairly hardy wee creatures. . ." He stopped. "*If* the storm holds off—*if* the baby is under shelter—*if* it is kept dry—*if* it is well wrapped up—*if* it is fed, even just water, enough to stop it dehydrating—it could survive through the night." Wallace felt his own lips go dry. He moistened them with his tongue. "Not much longer than that though."

"You've an awful lot of 'ifs' there, Doctor," said Dougal.

"Aye, I'm afraid so."

"And there's an awful lot of land up here to search," added Sergeant Murray. He rose from the table where he had been sitting, making notes. "I'd best go and see if we can raise Auchtarne on the radio." He walked to the door. "I hope your crofters get here soon, Dougal."

"They will," Dougal assured him. "Any time now."

And the Sergeant went out.

Wallace sat down heavily in the chair he had just vacated. His expression was serious. He looked up at Dougal with tired and weary eyes. He was their Doctor up here, but more than that—he was part of them and their lives. So much more than the folk down in Glendarroch and Auchtarne. He didn't know why. He wasn't born in Ardvain—it was just that he felt a great affinity with them. Their pain was his pain. "Dougal. . .," he said, very subdued.

"Aye," sighed Dougal. "I know, Doctor."

"Know what?" asked Morag.

Donald came toddling in from where he had been playing quietly in his grandmother's room. Morag gathered him up to her, but kept her question open.

"I've got to go to Bob Taylor's," said Dougal.

"Bob Taylor's?" queried Morag. "Why do you have to go to Bob's. . .?" And then it came to her. "*Alice*! Och, no, you don't think it's Alice, for goodness sake!"

"I don't know, Morag," Wallace said. "She's not been well, you see. Ever since she knew she could have no children of her own. . . It was a terrible disappointment to her. . ."

"I know all about it," exclaimed Morag, "but Alice would never in a million years do a thing like that. Aye, so she's not well—but she's the kindest, gentlest person. . . She could never take a baby away from its own mother. . . Never!" She looked at Dougal. "You know that!"

"Morag," said Dougal, "someone has the baby. Now if Alice was away over to see us here—she'd come by that road—she'd pass that car, wouldn't she? Think on it, Morag. There's a wean in the back seat cryin' its wee heart out—what is she going to do?"

"She'd bring it here, of course," said Morag. She looked at them both defiantly.

"I doubt it," Wallace said.

"Then it's safe in her place."

"Hopefully," the Doctor muttered.

The door to the other bedroom opened very quietly. Grace stood in the doorway and beckoned to Wallace. "The lass is stirring, Doctor," she said, almost in a whisper.

The Chicken Galantine had been a success, Elizabeth was sure. In fact, the whole luncheon seemed to have been thoroughly enjoyed by Sir Jeffrey. There had been no interruptions and the phone had been put on 'hold' by Lorna Seton. He and Elizabeth had talked on a dozen different subjects, none of which had been even remotely connected with Glendarroch Estate. They had many interests in common, a love of Victorian Landscapes, Regency Decor, Restoration Theatre, Rennaissance Music, roses, fine food and the glories of the Scottish glens, bens and lochs. They were traditionalists, unashamedly so: idealists, only tentatively so. Realists, certainly. They both knew the world was sometimes a grim and ugly place. The best one could hope for was to find occasional pools of grace and tranquillity hidden within it. And when they were discovered—they were to be shared and enjoyed.

But they had to be shared. Otherwise they became sterile selfish indulgences.

Sir Jeffrey was a widower. His wife had been the daughter of a famous distiller, extremely wealthy, incredibly beautiful, totally corrupt. She had died of drug abuse many years before addiction had become quite so commonplace. It was no secret, but it was treated as an embarrassing indiscretion—and had been curtained off from the light of day by polite society. Sir Jeffrey was certain that Elizabeth would have made extensive enquiries about his background. She would know all about his wife's unpleasant death. There was no need for either of them to speak of it.

They took their coffee cups to the window and stood looking out at the churning clouds. They were low and ominous, like a moving quilt descending over the landscape. Ben Darroch had already disappeared. Laird's Vantage was a looming silhouette and the loch was like a plate of dark pewter.

"Do you think we can still get to Ben Darroch before the storm hits?" asked Sir Jeffrey.

"Yes," answered Elizabeth. "If you want to. The rain won't come down until well after tea-time. Actually, Ben Darroch will look quite dramatic in this light. Very Wagnerian. Our German masters would be most impressed." She smiled. "I've always thought the Chairman, Hans Meier, had a penchant for the 'darkly Macabre'. Very 'Götterdamerung'. Very apocalyptical."

"Is he going to be difficult to do business with?" asked Sir Jeffrey. "Assuming that one *might* want to do business with him, of course."

"Very correct, I think." Elizabeth took a sip of her coffee.

"That puts him at a disadvantage. I'm rather devious when it comes to negotiating. Very prompt when it comes to settling bills, though."

"Oh, he'll be delighted about that. I think Frankfurt have a 'cash-flow' problem."

"Ah! That was rather indiscreet of you, Elizabeth," he admonished her. "Privileged information. I fear it was a little disloyal to your colleagues on the Board."

But Elizabeth seemed totally unconcerned. "Yes," she agreed, "I rather fear it was. But then I have always felt that my first allegiance was to Glendarroch—not to Frankfurt."

"You realise you are giving me an advantage over them?"

"Yes," she said.

He regarded her quietly for a moment or two, noting carefully that there was no coyness in her attitude. None whatsoever. Just coolness and an icy calm. "How much do you think they want for the entire Estate?" he asked.

"I'm not sure. But I can make an educated guess—a sophisticated estimate."

"Well?"

"I'll tell you after you've seen a little more of the Estate."

"Under the assumption, dear lady, that the more I see . ."

". . . the more you'll think it's worth."

"Are you certain of that?"

"I'm positive," she said.

Of all the people she had ever met, she felt that Sir Jeffrey Leighton-Fyffe was the one who might just match her own deep feelings for Glendarroch. Perhaps somewhere back in their mutual ancestry a Leigh Leighton or a Fyffe had stood with a Peddie by the lochside and watched its waters turn to pewter and laughed with excitement as storm clouds brewed over their heads.

On Ardvain the rain had begun to fall as the first of the crofters arrived at the Lachlans. They parked well back from the cottage, knowing that there was a sick woman inside. There was Robbie Moncur and Willie Tulloch, followed by Jamie Lockhart. They said that Hamish was on his way and that Tam Shaw had already headed off to the west to alert Hughie and Drew McNair, whilst his brother Bruce, had taken the Constable down to the phone box below Moncur's place. Even Morag's father, Jamie Stewart, using her old bicycle, had come over.

Every message had to be passed verbally, because there were no phones up on Ardvain and, unfortunately, the

Sergeant had been unable to raise Auchtarne on his police car radio. The Constable, when he called through to the Station, was going to have to get them to put a police car in Glendarroch to relay messages between Ardvain and Auchtarne.

No one, at this stage, knew just how big an operation this might turn out to be. If the search was going to be spread over most of Ardvain, then tracker dogs and helicopters might have to be brought onto the scene (although it seemed that the worsening weather might preclude the use of the latter for some time). Everything would have to be carefully coordinated from a central command, like a Mountain Rescue. By the time it was finished it would probably involve a lot of people.

In the interim, the lack of easy communiction between Ardvain and the outside world tended to isolate the story from the village's attention. It gave the Sergeant some breathing space and a chance to question each crofter as he arrived to help. He learnt from Robbie Moncur about the Forestry vehicle passing much earlier. Jamie Stewart said it had brought a couple of men up to do some fencing behind his place. It had gone back down again after it had dropped them off. No doubt it would come up later—at the end of their day's work. Morag believed one of them might be Brian Blair, she thought she had overheard Isabel mention something about a couple of days' work for him from the Forestry. The Sergeant made a note of that. Willie Tulloch wondered if they were using a pair of chain-saws on the fencing, because that might explain the noise he thought he heard later on, a sort of high-pitched whine, he said. Jamie Stewart maintained he hadn't heard anything that sounded like a chain-saw all morning, but then everyone knew that Jamie's hearing was not all that it used to be. . .

Whilst all this was going on it gave Dougal a chance to slip away in his Landrover and drive down to Bob Taylor's cottage. By now the rain was drumming on the roof of the cab and Dougal knew all the tracks and signs on the ground would soon be obliterated by the force of it. The conditions would continue to get worse and only the hardiest of the locals would be able to walk and search in it. Anyone else—especially a woman carrying a baby, say—would have a terrible time. The lashing rain could drive them into a bog or a flooding ditch—and drown them.

Bob's Estate Landrover was outside his cottage and even as Dougal drove up the front door opened and Bob came rushing out to greet him.

"Have you heard?" shouted Dougal over the hissing noise of the rain. He got down from the Landrover and ran over to Bob, who waved him inside. "Have you heard?" he repeated as the door closed behind.

There was really no need to ask. One look at Bob Taylor s face was enough. He was wild-eyed and scared. "Aye," he said. "Hamish McNeil drove down to the Darroch where I was working. . . He told me they'd found Moira Moncrieff unconscious in her car—and her baby gone." Bob could see Dougal staring about him, looking for some sign of Alice. Hoping against hope to see her— maybe in the kitchen, desperately wanting to hear her voice. "She's no' here, Dougal," said Bob, dully. "I've been back here an hour searchin' for her. She's nowhere about."

Dougal put a hand on his friends arm. "Hold on, man. It doesn't mean. . ." But Dougal stopped.

"It doesn't mean she found the car and took the baby?" asked Bob. "Is that what you were going to say, Dougal?"

"Aye, well. . ."

"Then why are you here?" Bob turned away in deep anguish. "No, you thought the same as me—straight away. She found a baby. She took it—*and God alone knows where they are now!*"

"If it was her—then you know she couldna' help hersel', Bob," said Dougal. "And we'll find them . . ."

"In this?" shouted Bob and he pointed to the window. "That's a right 'Ardvain Special' coming our way, Dougal! The wind will go mad and water will come down in buckets!"

"Do you know what she's taken with her? Can you tell what she was wearing?"

"Aye, her good mac's gone—and that wee holdall thing. . ."

"She took a bag?" said Dougal, interrupting.

"Aye—and her toothbrush and some toilet things. . . And her nightie."

"Then she came back!" said Dougal. "She must've done! I mean, she couldn't have just walked out of here wi' all her gear *expecting* to find Moira's baby on the road, could she?"

"What?" Bob looked confused.

"No," and Dougal's brain was racing. "She went out for a walk—maybe she was on her way up to see my mother—and she found the car and she heard the wean greetin' . . . So she took the baby out of the car and brought it back here. . ."

Bob picked up the thread. ". . .packed the holdall for herself—and took the baby off—where we'd not find her."

"And not take the baby from her, either. That's why she didn't come to our place."

"Oh, God," moaned Bob, "she's out there somewhere . ."

"Aye, but maybe not as far away as we thought. I'll have to get back and tell them, Bob. Weather's not going to get any better, lad." He could see Bob was getting ready to go with him. "Och, there's no need for you to come. . ."

"There's every need, Dougal. Sick or no'—she's my wife. I'm feared for here!" Even as he spoke both men were suddenly illuminated by an electric-blue flash of lightning and, as country folk often do, they instinctively started to count off the seconds that separated it from the inevitable roar of thunder that would follow. It would give them some idea of how fast the storm was travelling towards them now.

9

In the Shadow of Beinn Drimfern

Moira Moncrieff was drifting out of the blackness and into that strange limbo area of the semi-conscious mind where shapes were vague, sounds were wrapped in cotton-wool, memories non-existent and the only reality was the awesome throbbing pain in her head. Her eye-lids flickered, but the intermittent shafts of light they let in when they were open frightened her. There was someone close, she could sense that, but her arms were too heavy to lift and her body was a lump of immovable clay. She searched the void for a face—the face she needed—the nameless face *that had a name*, that had a smile, that had a passion and a body that was all embracing, awash with energy that hurt her, excited her, gave her life, poured life into her. . . "Andy—oh, my God, Andy you'll kill me! Oh, Andy. . . My Andy. . ." She tried hard to scream the name: "Andy!" But it came out as little more than a murmur.

" 'Andy'?" said Grace to Dr Wallace. "Was that 'Andy' she said?"

"Sounded like it." They were speaking in whispers. "What was the name of the baby?" asked Wallace.

"Morag said it was a wee girl. I don't know if she told me its name."

"Then maybe 'Andy' is the one the woman's looking for up here?"

"Andy?" Grace shook her head. "I don't know any 'Andy' up in Ardvain."

"She'll come round soon," said Wallace. "She'll be frightened and confused."

"Aye, and she'll ask for her baby—that'll be the first thing. What will we tell her?" asked Grace.

By the time Dougal and Bob Taylor got back to the Lachlan croft more men had arrived to help in the search, despite the weather. The MacDonalds had come over from Allt na Cala, father and son, and the Agnews, two brothers and a cousin, from Brig o' Foyle—they picked up Josh Stephenson on their way.

Brian Blair also showed up—alone. He had gone down

to Jamie Stewart's croft to get a bottle of water to top up their billican to make tea, using the old bicycle the Forestry had left them for emergencies. There had been no one at the Stewarts, Jamie had already left, so Brian cycled on to Tulloch's place. Mrs Tulloch was there—and she told him about the missing baby—and the search that would have to be organised to find it. Brian doubled back along the road pedalling as fast as he could, swerving the bike round the ruts and the potholes.

There were several hours of daylight left, but the quality of it was bad. The metallic sheen of the rain-driven atmosphere gave poor visibility and the terrain, rocky, gorse and heather covered, now becoming really soggy, would make walking, even for shepherds and crofters, very difficult.

Bob Taylor had gone straight to the Sergeant and told him about Alice—and his fears of what could have happened. These suspicions, of course, had to be relayed to the men who had come to help. There was nearly a score of them now, but they said nothing. They all knew Alice—knew, also, of the tragedy that had visited the Taylor cottage, the illness that had changed a quiet, but laughing girl, into an unhappy, haunted introvert.

Sergeant Murray was happy to leave the organising of the search to Dougal. He was the specialist. There was more than one tourist-hiker, who had braved Ardvain without adequate planning and advice, who now owed his life to Dougal's instinct and knowledge of this place.

If their assumption was correct, and Alice had returned to her home before setting out with the baby, then at least they had a starting point. Dougal's theory, fed by that instinct, was that she would be drawn towards the bulk of Beinn Drimfern, the most distinct landmark viewed from Taylor's back garden. It would act, Dougal thought, like a magnet, pulling her under its protection, offering her false sanctuary in amongst its treacherous shadows. Under these conditions Dougal knew she would never reach its skirt. There were marshes and peat bogs surrounding it that would drag her down, by now they would all be quagmires.

But there was shelter, too. The peak of Beinn Drimfern was nearly eight miles away and there were probably half a dozen ruined crofts between it and the stone wall that marked the boundary of Bob Taylor's back garden. With luck Alice and the baby might have reached one of them.

Dougal sent the men off in pairs, each pair with at least one dog between them. They would move out like the spokes of half a wheel, a fan, an arch with Bob's cottage as the hub, Beinn Drimfern as its keystone. As others arrived they would be directed to broaden the fan, open it out until it finally became a full 360 degree search. The Sergeant would remain at the Lachlans', at least until a more senior police officer took over, and ensured that those who came up from Glendarroch to help would have a crofter or a shepherd with them. The search would continue until an hour before nightfall. Everyone would return then. Hand flares and whistles were issued out to every pair of searchers. If the weather improved at all— then the RAF would send out their helicopters, but they would be wasted in the present visibility.

Dougal and Bob, with Tav at their heels, took that 'keystone' line—the direct line from the Taylor cottage to the peak of Beinn Drimfern.

They walked steadily for an hour, speaking very little, saving all their breath to fight the weather, leaning against the wind and rain, still counting the seconds (much fewer now) between the lightning flashes and the thunderclaps. Dougal worked Tav remorselessly, sending the young bitch out to investigate every hump and mound.

All three took their first breather as they reached the roofless walls of a long deserted croft. They went through the yawning doorway, looked anxiously about them—but found the place empty. They sank down in a corner, relishing the comparative calm, listening to the rain and wind drumming and screeching against their backs rather than straight into their faces.

Dougal had thought to bring a flask. He handed it first to Bob and as the Water Bailiff took a deep swig, Dougal glanced at the four walls. "This has always been known as Gloorie's Croft," he said, "though who the hell Gloorie was is anyone's guess now. It's been a ruin since anyone can remember."

Bob felt the whisky burn the back of his throat and then glow down to his stomach. He returned the flask to

Dougal. "Clearances?" he suggested.

Dougal tipped back his head and drank deep. "Ah," he gasped. Then he put the stopper back on the flask. "Or starvation," he said.

"Gloorie?" And Bob looked at the mute and battered walls afresh. "That's not a local name, is it?"

"No, neither's 'Glory'—and I doubt if that's what it stemmed from, anyway." Dougal rubbed the calf of his legs, bringing the circulation back to where the muscles were beginning to throb a little. You should never 'stop and squat', his old man used to say. And he was right. Dougal could walk for hour after hour in all conditions, over any terrain, providing he didn't stop and sit down for rest. "Mind you," he went on, "could be Irish. Some of them reached as far as here. Didn't stay long, I'm told." He laughed. "Maybe they couldn't stand the peace and quiet, eh?"

"Maybe not," said Bob. Nothing peaceful or quiet about today, though. There was a few moments of silence between them. Bob broke it. "Could Alice have got this far, Dougal?"

"I don't know."

"You've been searching the ground—have you seen any signs at all?"

"Och, it's like sponge rubber today, Bob. It would all have gone by now. . ."

"Man, you've got eyes like a hawk!" Bob said, impatiently. "If there was anything there—rain or no—you'd see it."

Dougal sighed. "I've seen nothing." He saw the desperation come into Bob's eyes. "Look, we're on just one line—one narrow line—you've no idea what the others may have come across."

"Aye," muttered Bob, unconvinced. "Aye, of course."

"Come on," said Dougal. He got to his feet, called to Tav, and held a hand out to help Bob up. "This is only the first hour. Even an orphan lamb could survive this wi' no trouble at all."

Bob nodded and took his hand. The storm was no worse, but it was no better either. They faced Beinn Drimfern and walked away from the meagre shelter of Gloorie's Croft.

The police, following the phone call from Murray's Constable, sent a radio car to Glendarroch, where they could relay calls from the Sergeant up in Ardvain. For the time being Auchtarne decided to leave him in charge of the operation. Sergeant Murray was a local man. The Senior Officer in Auchtarne, an Inspector, was a Glaswegian.

Murdoch had still been unable to contact Chisholm from the *Gazette*—but the events up in Auchtarne were no longer a secret. Molly MacPhearson had informed the Factor—and Dunbar was already rounding up volunteers to go and help with the search. Strangely enough, Archie Menzies was amongst the first to offer. Then Jimmy Blair and a couple of the lads from the Aqua Sports dropped everything, grabbed the Store van and headed up that ghastly road. Some of the farmers from outside the village rounded up their workers from sodden fields, but Alec Geddes and Fiona Cunningham had a better idea. They loaded Tamberlaine, and a strong mare called Belair, into the big horse box and drove very slowly as far as Moncur's croft. There they unloaded, saddled up and rode across country to report to the Sergeant at Lachlan's. They could cover twice the amount of ground and see more from the back of their horses than anyone on foot.

Ghillies and Estate workers joined the small throng heading northwards to search for Alice Taylor and Moira Moncrieff's missing baby. The Ardvain road, now a treacherous mud slide, had more traffic slithering up it than it had seen for many, many years.

Sir Jeffrey and Elizabeth Cunningham were totally unaware of all this activity. They were on the other side of the Estate, round by Ben Darroch and the grouse moors, cocooned in the plush quietness of the burgundy Rolls-Royce.

Moira had sunk slowly back down into the merciful black abyss of unconsciousness again, but Dr Wallace noted that her pulse was stronger and her respiration less erratic. He thought he could safely leave her in Grace's care for a minute or two whilst he had a look at conditons outside. He had to make a decision about the ambulance. The Cottage Hospital in Auchtarne had only one vehicle. If he called it out now to take Moira away—what would happen if it was suddenly needed when they found Alice or

Moira's baby? He could call for another ambulance from Inveraray, but that was a really long and arduous journey— and Alice or the baby might need a life or death dash to hospital. It might take far too long to get it up to Ardvain and then down to the Cottage Hospital in Auchtarne. For the time being Moira was probably safer in the croft than being shuttled down to Auchtarne on a stretcher in the back of a swaying ambulance—especially if she had regained consciousness and knew she was being taken farther and farther away from her missing baby.

Wallace came out of the Lachlans' front door and immediately turned up his coat collar against the driving rain. The police car was parked a few yards away and he could make out Sergeant Murray sitting in the front, talking to the relay car on the radio. Wallace ran over and the Sergeant opened the door for him.

". . .Thank you, Delta Bravo. Listening and out." The Sergeant switched the radio to stand-by as Wallace settled in the passenger seat beside him. "They're still not keen to scramble the search 'copter," he said. "The weather all round us is even worse. I suppose He's letting us know the summer's over, eh?" And the Sergeant nodded heavenwards. "How's the woman, Doctor? You want the ambulance called yet? We can probably patch you through to the Cottage Hospital. . .".

"No," said Wallace. "I don't want to call out the ambulance yet. The woman regained consciousness for a little while—but she's drifted off again. Still, she seems to be improving. She mentioned the name 'Andy' a couple of times: mean anything to you?"

"Well, there's a couple of Andys down in Glendarroch."

"No, I'd say she was looking for him up here."

The Sergeant tugged at his ear-lobe. "Andy?" he mused. "Common enough name, but I don't think there are any 'Andys' up here just now. Last one I remember was old man Finlayson's father—yes, he was Andy Finlayson—but they're both dead. Andy Finlayson passed on when I was a lad. Maybe she was mistaken, Doctor. Maybe she only *thinks* this fellow she's looking for lives up here, eh? Maybe she's on the wrong track?"

"Aye, maybe she is, but until we can talk to her we shan't know, shall we?"

"The assumption is that one of our Ardvain crofters is the father of the baby," said the Sergeant. "According to Morag Stewart, the lass is a barmaid at a pub they use when they go down to the Lanark Market." Once again he tugged at the lobe of his ear. "Bit awkward if that crofter was a married man, eh?"

"Awkward for Moira Moncrieff, too," grunted Wallace.

They were silent for a moment. The Sergeant coughed. He was staring at the tiny 'stand-by' light on his radio. "You think Alice Taylor has taken the kid, Doctor?"

"That's an assumption, too. But it seems a fairly logical one, given Alice's present state of mind. Women under pressure do these things, you know."

"Men, under pressure, sometimes do worse things," said the Sergeant very quietly. Even in Auchtarne he had seen some violence and savagery. The taint of the 'boot-and-knife' madness had reached even to them. Sometimes Sergeant Iain Murray was shocked at his own sullied mind and vicious suspicions. He could remember when it didn't used to be like that.

"Men?" asked Wallace. "What do you mean?"

"Supposing," said the Sergeant, hesitantly, "just supposing Alice Taylor didn't take the baby. Supposing someone else found them. Supposing someone else was waiting for them—maybe ambushed the car on that bend. Not difficult—there was fog and mist, wasn't there? It's the tightest bend till you get past Tulloch's turn-off. . ."

"Hey, hold on, Sergeant," said Wallace. "What the hell are you talking about?"

"Assumptions, Doctor. Alternatives."

"Alright, go on."

"Supposing our unknown father heard she was coming up? She had planned the trip yesterday—but her car was on the blink. Ken Calder came out from Auchtarne to fix it. So, up here, they knew Moira Moncrieff was in Glendarroch. They knew she'd probably make it today."

Wallace stared at the man next to him. "Sergeant, you are suggesting that the father took that baby—and. . . And *what?*"

"He might have killed it," said the Sergeant, unemotionally. "If he was married, if he had a family up here—and enough to lose. He might have lifted the kid from the back seat, whilst Moira Moncrieff was unconscious, taken it away—killed it—and buried it somewhere." The Sergeant stared out of the window. "In this weather we'd never find the grave."

"Sergeant, people around here don't do that sort of thing," insisted Wallace, horrified, even as a doctor, at the very thought.

"Don't they?" Murray returned his gaze to the little green light on the radio. "Brian Blair battered a girl to death in Glendarroch twelve years ago. And, come to think of it, Brian Blair is up here today."

"For God's sake, Brian Blair doesn't go to the Lanark Market! He couldn't possibly *know* Moira Moncrieff!"

"You said people around here don't do that sort of thing. I was just pointing out that they do, Doctor." He nodded slowly, as though agreeing with himself. "I'm afraid they do."

"I just hope you're way off the mark!"

"I just hope *your* assumption's the right one," added the Sergeant. "I hope Alice Taylor *did* take the baby. At least she'll try and protect it, won't she?"

"She'll try. But she'll be distraught. In reasonable weather I'm sure it would only be a question of time before we located her. In this, though. . .?" Wallace looked at the pelting rain through the windscreen. "I'm not making any more assumptions."

Even across the sound of the wind they heard the scream. It started as the croft door opened and Morag was beckoning to Wallace urgently.

"Your patient, Doctor?" said the Sergeant.

"Sounds like it." Wallace opened the car door.

"If she's well enough to answer a few questions. . ."

"I'll let you know, Sergeant." And Wallace sprinted for the open croft door. The screaming had stopped.

In fact, Moira was alright. Just very frightened for the moment. She had climbed out of that abyss for the second time, swimming out of the blackness too quickly. It was the shock that had caused the involuntary scream of terror. She didn't know where she was, nor what had happened to her. But Grace had calmed her down by the time Wallace entered the tiny room—and Moira's memory had come flooding back. It was frightening for her, but it was a good sign. The lack of amnesia seemed to indicate that there was no serious damage, even though her head ached abominably. "My baby!" she shouted. "Where's Lilian?" She grabbed Grace by the arm. "Oh, dear God, she's not hurt?"

"Now, you're to lay back and relax, lass," said Grace, soothingly. "Och, look at you. You're in no state to have your wean here with you just now, are you? This is Dr Wallace and you've to let him check you over first: d'you hear me, Moira?"

"Yes." The voice was calmer, the wild panic leaving her.

Grace stepped back to let Wallace come to the bedside. He smiled at Moira reassuringly.

Finally, late in the afternoon, Murdoch got through to Chisholm. The newspaperman, befuddled by Lord Glengowrie's hospitality, took some time to sort out just what it was that Murdoch was talking about. Then the bargaining took longer than the relaying of the actual story. Murdoch settled for eight pounds, plus fifty pence to cover the cost of his constant phone calls during the day.

However, once Chisholm got the gist of it his head seemed to clear miraculously. He grabbed a young photographer who could drive—and called through to a national daily in London (he didn't want the Glasgow dailies to pip him to the post) and negotiated a coverage deal with them which made Murdoch's eight pounds look very silly. Chisholm was an old campaigner. He could smell a good story a mile off, even with a pint and a half of red wine sloshing about in his stomach. This one was going to make headlines, providing they didn't find that missing baby too quickly. If it had not been for Chisholm's over-fondness for alcohol he could have been a top-line journalist.

He could feel his pulse race with excitement as he saw the police car parked on the verge by the T-junction that led into Glendarroch village. Despite the rotten weather he saw women huddled together in little groups in their doorways, muttering quietly, earnestly, the way they always do when there is a disaster or a tragedy close by.

Chisholm could not believe his luck when he sensed that there were no other newspapermen around. He decided he might be generous and give Murdoch the ten pounds he originally asked for.

The fog and mists had long ago dispersed, but the swirling clouds were very low and black. The wind and rain had in no measure abated. Even so, the RAF had decided to try a brief helicopter sweep of the Beinn Drimfern area. The police realised that time was now very much against them. They needed to find some sign of Alice and the baby before the last hours of daylight ran out on them. The RAF agreed it was worth the risk.

Over on the grouse moors, by Ben Darroch, Sir Jeffrey and Elizabeth watched the helicopter battle its way through the storm. They gave it little more than a fleeting glance, but Sawyer, in the driving seat of the Rolls, had done his National Service in the Royal Air Force as a maintenance engineer—and he wondered what sort of an emergency it could be that would bring a Rescue 'Copter out in this lousy weather.

The visibility was so bad that Elizabeth suggested that they call it a day. Sir Jeffrey would just have to extend his visit in the hope that the weather would improve over the next day or two. The idea obviously did not displease him.

Elizabeth guided Sawyer along the back roads from Ben Darroch that would take them to the Dower House without having to go through the village.

For the time being, therefore, they were destined not to see the police car—or the groups of women huddled in the doorways, looking anxiously towards Ardvain.

And, for the time being, Arthur Chisholm would miss seeing the burgundy Rolls-Royce and Sir Jeffrey Leighton-Fyffe.

10

Stormbreak

"Alright, this is as far as we go, Bob," said Dougal. The walking was really bad now and their boots were squelching deep into the sticky clay with every step.

"Aw, come on," urged Bob, shouting out the words against the squalling wind, "there's still plenty of time, man! We can go on a while yet." To Bob it seemed that the brooding bulk of Beinn Drimfern was no nearer. If he allowed his imagination to override his commonsense, he could believe it was, if anything, farther away.

"Oh, we can go on," agreed Dougal, gazing about him, "but it'll not do any good. And we've to get home yet. We'll move due west for half a mile and then head back to your cottage, keeping Beinn Drimfern to our backs the while." He turned to the new direction and took a couple of steps before Bob grabbed at him.

"Dougal, there are some more ruined crofts under Beinn Drimfern, no more than a mile away," said Bob, desperately. "You mind we stalked that old stag up by there a couple of years ago. . ."

"Alice wouldna ha' got this far, Bob—let alone any farther—not with the ground in the state it's in. Use your head. If she's carrying a baby and that holdall thing—she'd be walking at a third of the speed we've been travelling. If she had come this way, we would have overtaken her an hour back." Dougal turned to look at Beinn Drimfern. "Maybe I was wrong. Maybe she went in the opposite direction—away from it."

Suddenly they heard the unique 'swish-clatter' sound of helicopter blades and saw the machine swooping low, dangerously low, over the smaller braes behind them. Obviously the pilot was having great difficulty identifying anything on the ground. It circled a couple of times and then lurched off towards the southwest.

"They should have had that thing up hours ago!" said Bob.

"They wouldn't've known what to look for hours ago," Dougal answered. "I'm not sure they know now."

"Just one woman carrying a bairn in her arms. . ."

"Have you seen any flares, Bob?"

"No. Why?"

They began plodding on. Dougal whistled for Tav, but he could see the bitch was tiring, too. "There must be a score or more of crofters out searching by now—with maybe twice that number of folk from Glendarroch, plus whatever policemen Auchtarne and Inveraray have sent us. Now I hold no great store by the villagers or the policemen, they don't know this place—but the ghillies and the crofters—they should have spotted something by now. There should have been a signal flare, Bob. Alice is just a wee lass—and not a great walker." He shrugged. "Then neither was her sister, Amy." He watched Tav lope away to check a gorse-thick fold to their left. "Alice couldna have gone any distance at all!"

"Then where the devil is she?" shouted Bob, as a new and stronger gust of wind tore the words from his mouth.

"Save your breath for walking, Bob," said Dougal. He thought a 'break' in the storm might be close. If it was they would have a short lull, a respite as the weird phenomena opened up over them. There would be a strange oasis of calm whilst the wind and rain gathered strength for their final onslaught, whipping them, next time, from the opposite direction. Dougal could feel the downdraught of cold air that signalled the approach of a 'stormbreak'. Unfortunately, it would not last long, Other crofters would have sensed it, too. If it came before nightfall, the pilot of the helicopter, *if* he was still flying, would get a far better view of the terrain below him.

Bob took Dougal's advice and saved his breath for walking: the effort was making him gasp now, and he needed every ounce of air he could drag down into his lungs, but his thoughts raced on wildly. Where *was* Alice? What *had* happened to her?

And in his mind Bob conjured up an awful vision of Alice, clutching the wailing child in one arm, the wretched holdall in the other, sinking down, down into some ghastly peat-bog, calling his name, screaming for help—until the ooze filled her mouth and even her head disappeared from view. . .

". . . Mrs MacPhearson said the road was bad—but I didn't realise it was *that* bad," said Moira. She was talking quietly, rationally to Dr Wallace. She had not asked again about the baby, probably assuming that it was being cared for by Morag, who had brought in some tea for them. Tea was such a normal thing: warm, sweet tea—comforting, like gentle, motherly Grace Lachlan—reassuring, like the Doctor. "Oh, I could have managed alright, even the sharp bends and the potholes—they ought to do something about yon potholes—but it was the fog and mist patches that scared me. You were into them before you knew. And that damn' road seemed to go on forever. . . And I couldn't find any of the croft cottages. . ." She took another sip of the tea. She was sitting up in the big bed and the large bruise on her temple was turning livid, an ugly amalgam of yellow and purple that contrasted with the pure whiteness of the pillowcase behind her. "Aye, and then there was this really sharp bend coming up—and wee Lilian woke and started to cry. . . I remember the bend was covered in fog, it was like going into a wall of grey cotton-wool. . ." She put her fingers up to the bruise. They were trembling at the memory and Wallace watched her carefully. "And there was something *inside* that patch of fog, Doctor! *There was something in there.*"

"Did you see what it was, Moira?" Wallace asked.

"Something whiteish, y'ken? Like a giant sheet floatin'—but fast!" And Moira was frightened again. "Roaring and comin' straight at me!"

"A sheet? Floating? Roaring?"

"I saw this documentary once—on telly— one of those underwater things—maybe by Jacques Cousteau. . . Was that his name? Anyway, they showed you sharks and octopuses and beautiful coral reefs and a' that. And there was this horrible thing called a giant ray—like a great sheet moving through the water. God, it was enormous—and it moved as fast as an express train. . . Only, in the film it was silent. Aye, it was something like that I saw. As big as that. . . Och, I dunno. That was the impression I got. . . Maybe it was my imagination, eh? I stamped on the brake as hard as I could. The wheels locked, I think. And I spun." She closed her eyes. "And that's all I remember. . ."

"Moira," said Wallace, very quietly.

"Aye?"

"Who's Andy? Is he the father of your baby?"

"Aye. That's why I'm here. I heard them talking in the bar one night. They let it slip—he's an Ardvain crofter. Ardvain. . ." She savoured the name and smiled. "It sounded so nice and peaceful. I thought he should see his wee daughter. Och, I didn't want to make trouble for him, honest. But I needed to talk to him. . . Find out what he wanted for the bairn."

"We've been racking our brains, Moira," Wallace said, carefully, not wanting to upset her again, "but we can't think of an 'Andy' living up this way."

"Oh, don't fret, Doctor," she said, casually. " 'Andy's' probably not his real name. If they think they're going to get into your bed—they don't give their proper names. And at the 'Crawford' they all thought they would get me between the sheets before they left." She gazed up at Wallace unashamedly. "Only one of them ever did. 'Just call me 'Andy' he said. "Aye, and just call me 'Muggins', said I". She lowered her eyes. "But he was kind and he was gentle—and he was lovin', Doctor. He was no' a rowdy—and he wasna' drunk, either. I've no complaints. I'd just like to talk to him again."

"And if he's married?"

"I'll tell his wife I'm a poor wee widow-woman, on holiday, visiting all her good bar guests from Glendarroch and Ardvain. Couldn't resist seeing the place, I'll tell her, after all the nice things they said about the countryside up here. That's what I'll say—if he has a family."

"And then go back to Lanark?" asked Wallace.

"No. Not Lanark. Maybe I'll go on up to Oban and get a job. I'm a good barmaid, Doctor, for a' that. We're usually in demand." She looked from Wallace to Grace, who had been standing quietly in the corner. "May I have my baby back now, please?" Moira asked.

Some of the searchers had already come back in and gone off again on a different tack. Others had returned and were resting.

Though the hub of the search remained Taylor's cottage, the 'operational centre' was Lachlan's croft. More police had arrived, but Sergeant Murray remained in charge. Mrs Tulloch and Willie's two daughters bicycled down and, together with Morag, they were serving out tea from the

'beaters' urn, brought up by Archie Menzies and the
Factor from Glendarroch House, together with tea, milk,
sugar and mugs.

But there had been no sign of Alice, no sightings at all.
The really experienced walkers and stalkers of Ardvain,
men like Josh Stephenson, Hamish McNeil, the Agnews
and Jamie Stewart, had seen no evidence of her, either. It
was as though Alice and the baby had vanished into thin
air.

Brian Blair came in exhausted, wet, mud-splattered and
miserable. He had been out with one of the Estate ghillies, a
man a dozen years older than Brian, but whose legs
seemed to grow longer and younger by the mile, whilst his
had started to ache and stiffen after the first few hundred
yards. Gratefully he took a mug of tea from Morag, found
a corner of Lachlan's yard and squatted down on his own,
using the side of Dougal's barn to shelter him from the
worst of the weather. He wrapped his gloved fingers
around the mug and sipped at the scalding tea.

"Hell, man but you look rough."

Brian looked up and saw that Sergeant Murray had
found him. The Policeman stood, hands in pockets, peaked
cap dripping with the rain, looking down on him.

"It's no' exactly a summer ramble out there, Sergeant,"
said Brian, morosely.

"Good of you to help, though."

Brian closed his eyes wearily. He could almost sense
what the Sergeant was after. "Least we can do, isn't it?" he
muttered.

"How did you hear about the missing baby, Brian?" the
Sergeant asked.

"I'm sure you know."

"How would I know, Brian?"

"Because as soon as you found I was here—you'd ask
around."

"Oh, is that what I'd do, eh? Why?"

"You know why, Sergeant," said Brian.

"Because you're the only 'hard man' we have in the
area?"

There was a cynical edge to the Sergeant's voice. It was the
edge he used when he was questioning suspects. "Because
you're the only man with a record for violence in the

district? The only one who's served ten years for murder? Would that be why I'd ask around, Brian?"

"I suppose so."

"Aye, so now let me hear it from you: how did you hear about the missing baby?"

Brian took a deep breath and watched some spots of rain drive their way into his mug of tea. "I'm doing some fencing for the Forestry, behind Jamie Stewart's place. I wanted fresh water to make a brew so I cycled down with a bottle to Jamie's cottage. There was no one there. So I went to the road and on to Mrs Tulloch's. She told me."

"And you came straight to help look for Alice Taylor and the baby?"

"Yes."

"Anything wrong, Dad?" the voice belonged to Jimmy. He had seen Sergeant Murray walk over and talk to his father. He knew the anguish and anger Brian would be experiencing if Murray was questioning him. The anger that had to be suffered in silence. He knew the shame his father would feel as others saw the policeman there. They would—and did—nudge each other, speculating on whether or not a new element had crept into the mystery of the missing baby.

"Nothing wrong, son," said Brian, looking up at Jimmy. "Is there, Sergeant?"

"I hope not," said Murray. "Oh, just one more thing," and he added: "for the minute, that is."

"Sergeant, do you have to persecute my father every time anything goes wrong around here?" Jimmy retorted angrily.

"It's alright, Jimmy, I'm used to it," he lied.

The Sergeant ignored the interruption, but he took his hands out of his pockets. "I was saying—there's just one more thing: have you been using a chain-saw up on that fence?"

"Chain-saw? No. The posts are all cut." Brian returned his attention to the mug in his hands. "But I'm belting them into the ground, Sergeant. I'm using a sledge-hammer—if you're thinking about deadly weapons!"

"So it wasn't a chain-saw Willie Tulloch heard earlier on," mused the Sergeant.

"I don't know what you're talking about," said Brian.

The Sergeant looked around the yard at the groups of searchers, some of them quite animated, talking earnestly, others huddled exhausted against the walls of Dougal's outhouses. "Good, isn't it?" said Murray. "All these people turning up in this weather, wanting to help. Crofters, villagers—most of the able bodied men from the Estate. . ." he nodded. "Aye, it's good. Even the two lads who work for you, eh, Jimmy—Robbie and Alistair—I see they came with you."

"Everyone wants to help, Sergeant—*including* my father."

"But none of your tourists, eh? None of the young folk from your Aqua Sports?" said the Sergeant. "Mostly gone, I suppose?"

"Yes, Sergeant."

"Back to their big houses and rich parents?"

"They didn't all have big houses and rich parents," Jimmy pointed out, curtly. "Some of them saved all year for their holiday on Loch Darroch!"

"They didn't give you any trouble, did they, Sergeant?" Brian asked.

"No, no. None at all," said Murray. Then he tugged at his ear lobe. "Well, there was just one wee incident."

"What 'incident'?" asked Jimmy.

"Couple of my constables chased a lass in a sports car along the Auchtarne Road. They said she was hitting the ton. Couldn't have been though. Our Panda would never have got near her. Good driver, they said, but going too fast. They had to give her a caution. But that's all. No other trouble. I expect they're all too exhausted after their water skiing to stir up anything." Murray smiled. "Mind you," he said, "I must say they were a good looking bunch of kids this year. Oh, some of those lasses, Brian. Right bobby-dazzlers, especially that one in the sports car, according to my constables." He stared at Brian, watching for some reaction. "D'you not agree, man?" He was obviously goading Brian—and Jimmy could see the tension tugging at the muscles round his father's mouth. And that nerve at his temple was beginning to jump.

"Yes," Brian spoke through taut lips. "Yes, Sergeant Murray, a good looking bunch of kids this year." His hands holding the mug were trembling with rage, making the surface of the tea dance.

"Especially some of the lasses—that one in the car, Brian. . ."

Jimmy cut in quickly, angrily, with: "That one would have been a blonde called Jeannie Roxburgh, Sergeant— and I was dating her. I don't suppose my father even spoke to her!"

The Sergeant relented. "No," he agreed. "Maybe not." He turned his attention from Brian back to Jimmy. "Oh, you were dating her, were you? Lucky young devil. Swop you jobs next summer, Jimmy?"

Jimmy stared hard at Murray. "Sergeant," he said, scathingly, but very precisely, "I wouldn't have your job— or your cesspit of a mind—for all the tea in China!"

Brian got quickly to his feet and put a restraining hand on Jimmy's arm. "Listen, hold on, Jimmy, for God's sake," he urged desperately, panic putting a tremor in his voice, "no trouble, please. . ."

But the Sergeant was calm, seemingly unworried. "It's alright, Brian," he said, still smiling. "It's alright. Loyalty's a good thing to have in a son. Very commendable. There's a lot of Isabel in him, isn't there?" The Sergeant gave them both a reassuring nod, then turned and walked slowly back towards his police car. Once again his thumb and forefinger tugged at the lobe of his ear. He was wondering whether or not to cross Brian Blair off his small list of 'assumptions and alternatives'. He knew he had failed to prod a definite reaction out of him—but he had sensed the violence lying just under the surface, ready, perhaps, to erupt like the compressed fire and energy of a volcano. The Blair temper that had exploded twelve years ago to smash and crush the life out of a girl who had goaded him too far—could it, in some strange, black way, be linked with the disappearance of Alice Taylor and a three month old little baby? Was that conceivable? Could quiet, timid Alice impel anyone to violence?

Sergeant Iain Murray was 'an old time copper'. There were aspects of the job he hated, like not being able to leave Brian Blair in peace, having to hound him like that. The man had enough troubles without becoming an immediate suspect for every crime, large or small, that occurred on this patch. No it wasn't fair—but Murray wished he was a postman. Either that—or that he could project himself four years onwards—when he would be out of uniform and drawing his pension. Maybe then he could have a pint of beer with Brian Blair—aye, and his plucky lad, Jimmy, and talk about cabbages and kings, rather than suspect and probe and ask for alibis. . .

Murray was tired, he was too old for this grind and pressure—and the damn' storm sapped all the energy from his weary mind and body. Especially his mind. He knew he was missing something. He knew he held a vital mini-piece of information, no more than a scrap—but he could not pinpoint it, could not drag it to the surface. A couple of years ago it would have leapt out at him. Now it was too elusive. A wraith—as intangible as the mists that had lain across Ardvain hours ago: the fogs and mists that had been dispersed by the pounding rain. . . It would come to him, eventually—but he hoped it would not come too late.

He looked up at the clouds and saw the 'break' the crofters had already sensed was coming. No more than a glow over to the north—but it was there, a little breathing space before the stormclouds covered it again. It would be followed, soon enough, by total darkness as the night crept in on them.

Moira Moncrieff was sobbing quietly; shuddering, gentle little sobs that squeezed the tears from her eyes until they coursed down her cheeks in ever moving droplets. Grace had an arm about Moira's shoulders, comforting her, murmuring words of reassurance that the old woman knew were no more than a temporary, hollow balm. They had told her, as carefully, as sensitively as they could, that her baby was missing. They had tried to suggest that someone had taken Lilian to safety after the crash—and that she would be found. Wallace told her that there was no evidence to prove that the baby was hurt. There was no blood, no ominous disarray or shattering of the cot.

Moira absorbed it all—controlling the hysteria, but not the tears. Wallace could give her no sedative to soothe her, not until he knew the extent of her head injury. She had been unconscious for a long time, but he felt sure that there was no serious damage. He was almost certain that it was just concussion, no more—but he could not take the risk of letting her slip into a drug induced sleep, from

whence he may not be able to bring her back. Cruel
though it may be, he knew that even the terrible turmoil
she was experiencing now was—therapeutic. It was of very
little consolation to him—and, if she had known—it would
have been even less consolation to Moira.

Back at Dower House, outside Glendarroch, Sir Jeffrey
Leighton-Fyffe stood at the french windows and gazed up
at the sky. From the depth of an armchair Elizabeth
watched him. They had been back from Ben Darroch and
the grouse moors for nearly an hour; however the time
had tip-toed past unheeded by them. Mrs Sawyer had
made tea and they had chatted about the moors, the cover
and the access to the area. They had not had a chance to
see very much, but the scenery, covered, as it seemed by a
muslin veil of rain and mist, had impressed Sir Jeffrey.

"I may be wrong," he said, "but I rather think this
wretched weather is coming to an end. Wind's dropping
a bit and the clouds are thinning."

"I'm afraid it's only a 'break'," said Elizabeth. "It's
something we get up here. A late summer storm will just
'break' for a little while. The rain will stop, the sky will
clear, the wind will drop to nothing. And then it all starts
up again."

"Really?"

"But there's one consolation. At least we know we're
halfway through it."

"Like an interval, eh?"

In the hall the phone rang and they heard Sawyer move
to answer it. They both found the sound an intrusion.

"It won't be for me," Sir Jeffrey said. "No one else
knows I'm here."

"There was a knock on the door and Sawyer came in.
"Excuse me, Sir, it's Mrs Cunningham's office on the
telephone."

Sir Jeffrey glanced at his watch. "Packing up time, I
suppose."

"They wouldn't leave a message?" asked Elizabeth.

Sawyer shook his head. "It was a Miss Lorna Seton. She
asked if she might speak to you."

"Will you excuse me, Sir Jeffrey?"

He gave a little bow. "With deep reluctance."

Elizabeth smiled, rose from the armchair and went into the hall. Sawyer closed the door to the lounge after her and indicated the waiting phone. Then he withdrew towards the kitchen area as Elizabeth put the receiver to her ear.

"Yes, Lorna?" she said.

"Oh, Mrs Cunningham, I'm awful sorry to disturb you." Lorna was trying hard to control her voice.

"What's happened?"

"Is there anyone close by? Can anyone hear you?" asked Lorna.

"No. What's wrong?"

"We've trouble here, Mrs Cunningham. There's been an accident up on Ardvain—there's a baby missing and the police think Alice Taylor may have taken it. . ." The calm and efficient Lorna was beginning to gabble.

"Alright, Lorna, take it steadily, please. There's a baby missing? They think Alice Taylor took it? And the police are up on Ardvain?"

"Yes. And down here in the village. There's also Arthur Chisholm, the reporter from the *Gazette*, here, too! He's been talking to Murdoch and Mrs Mack!"

Elizabeth was immediately concerned for the unknown missing baby—and for the fate of Alice Taylor—but she was also worried about Arthur Chisholm. No Press, Sir Jeffrey had stipulated. No Press at all. No hint as to his real reason for being in Glendarroch. No attention whatsoever to be drawn to him.

"Oh, God," whispered Elizabeth.

11

Crescendo

The silence was eerie. It rolled over the landscape like something tangible, something you could almost touch. It was the sudden absence of the whistling wind and the drumming rain. You no longer had to shout above the din—and you could hear yourself breathe. The clouds had pulled back to show—not a blue sky—but a pink-hued wash. The stormbreak was a time for collecting the tangled threads of jangled minds and weaving them back into recognisable patterns. It was an entr'acte, a mini-respite in which to brace yourself for the other half of the storm.

Wallace was waiting patiently at the police car, waiting for Sergeant Murray to finish his progress report, before asking if he could speak to his Surgery in Auchtarne through the police radio. Wallace's partner would be there by now, coping quite competently he was sure, but he liked to know what was happening, liked to keep in touch.

Morag came into the bedroom to sit with Moira Moncreif whilst Grace went to her kitchen to relax for a minute or two. It was less than two years ago since Grace herself had a heart attack and Morag was worried in case the pressure of all this worry and excitement might not bring on another. She suggested that Grace might make herself a cup of tea and put her feet up—just for a little while.

Moira was past caring who was with her now. She was reliving, over and over again, those last seconds before she went into that mist-shrouded bend, she was listening to Lilian crying—over and over again. . .

Grace was at the kitchen window, staring out, kettle in hand, when she saw him. He was in the yard, away from the rest, a forlorn figure, cap in hand, gazing at the curtained bedroom window. He was probably trying to pluck up enough courage to come and knock at the Lachlan's front door. Grace hadn't seen him, or the rest of his family, for many months. "Drew McNair," she called, "come on in here, my lad." He looked startled and confused, but did as he was told.

Grace filled the kettle as she heard her front door open quietly. "My boots are awful muddy, Mrs Lachlan. . ." he said.

"Then take them off at the door." As she turned off the tap she saw that wee Donald was out in the yard with one of the Tulloch girls, enjoying the novelty of being with so many people. Grace was pleased to see that Morag had thought to wrap the boy up well. She switched on the kettle and reached up for the tea caddy from the shelf. "Bad business, eh, Drew?" she said, without turning.

"Aye, Mrs Lachlan." His voice was very hushed.

Grace liked the McNairs but she saw them only very rarely. They lived too far over to the west, right at the very edge of the Estate. Pleasant, considerate family, Grace thought. Never any trouble. Drew was the youngest, twenty-seven years old; his brother, Hughie, was thirty and still courting the same Inveraray lass he met four or five years ago. There was talk that they might wed next year. His mother hoped so. Their father had died in the 'flu epidemic when both lads were still at school. She could use help now in the croft. Drew had no one—not until now. He was the shy one. Shy and sensitive, his mother said—but always thoughtful. And caring. Good looking lad too. Good eyes, Grace noticed. "You want some tea, Drew?" she asked.

"No, thank you, Mrs Lachlan. I had some from the urn." He looked towards the closed bedroom door. "Thank you all the same."

There was a silence then. Drew waited patiently.

"She was calling for you earlier," said Grace. "When she first stirred—she called for you. Took me a while to think on who 'Andy' was. Och, then I remembered. 'Andy'—'Andrew': that was your given name. Aye, Andrew. But it was 'Drew' your ma called you, because you were named after your dad—and she called him 'Andy'. Less confusing, eh? So you told the lass you were Andy."

"I—I didna' mean to lie to her," he said. "And it wasna' really a lie, was it?"

"No, I suppose not."

"I didna' even know she was having a baby, Mrs Lachlan."

Grace smiled sadly. "No, and I don't suppose she did, either. Not until it was too late."

"It wasn't just . . ." He was struggling to explain. Obviously it was important to him. "I liked her, you see. I

mean, I *really* liked her, Mrs Lachlan. I wanted to see her
again: but I didna know what she thought of me. . ." He
looked wretched and unhappy, but, most of all, he looked
confused.

"She thought enough to come lookin' for you, lad,"
sighed Grace. "Not to make trouble, y'ken—just to let you
see the wee baby—and talk to you. Can you imagine what
she's going through now, Drew— She's lost that wean,
she's amongst strangers, she's hurt and very frightened."

"Would it help if I went in to see her, Mrs Lachlan?"

"That depends," mused Grace.

"On what?"

"On how you treated her when you went in there, what
you said to her. It would depend on whether you were
nice and carin'—and, perhaps, made her feel just a wee bit
less scared, eh, Drew?"

"That's how I'd be, Mrs Lachlan," he said sincerely.
"Honest." He looked to the door again. "But what's going
to happen to her—afterwards? I mean, if they find the
baby. . .? Or if they dinna'? What's going to happen to
Moira?"

"Well, now, Drew McNair, my lad, I'd say that was very
much up to you." She nodded towards the door. "Morag
Stewart's in there. Tell her to come out and have a cup of
tea with me." She watched him walk slowly across the
room. "Oh and Drew, nice and carin' and gentle, mind.
She's been through a lot."

"Come on, Dougal," Bob urged, impatiently. "Let's get out
there again. We could head off towards Reiver's Gap. There
are some places there she could shelter. . ."

Dougal shook his head slowly. They had come back to
Dougal's place, via Bob's cottage. They had found no sign,
nothing. Most of the other searchers were back now, too.
The 'break' was still holding and, of course, for the
moment, the visibility was excellent. No one had seen
anything. "Waste of time," said Dougal.

"Hey, listen, it's my Alice we're talkin' on!" said Bob
angrily. "Your own sister-in-law! She's out there somewhere—wi' that wee bairn. . ."

"I doubt it," replied Dougal. "Wherever she is—I doubt
if she's on Ardvain, Bob." He indicated the quiet groups of

tired men standing around the yard, waiting for news—or the next move. "Look at all these folk here. They know this ground, they've a feel for it, man. They'd find a sick ewe buried in a snowdrift five miles away from the rest of the flock in mid winter: do you think they could have missed Alice? She's only been gone a few hours?"

"Then where the hell did she go, Dougal?"

"By road. Someone gave her a lift—either back down to Glendarroch—or way over to the west, past McNairs and on to Inveraray," said the crofter quietly. "That's my guess."

"But we've checked every vehicle. . ."

"No. We haven't, Bob."

And even as he spoke the Forestry truck that brought Brian Blair and his workmate up that morning was returning now to take them back home. It pulled into the yard and parked close to the police car. Dougal and Bob hurried over to it, but Sergeant Murray had got there before them. It gave Dr Wallace a chance to use the police radio and check with his Surgery.

The Forestry driver, Davy Fergus, got out from behind the wheel and nodded to Murray. "Right business, eh, Sergeant?" he said.

"D'y'ken what's happened, Davy?" the Sergeant asked.

"Well, they say there's a wee bairn missin' up here. . . I heard it from Glendarroch and I saw a Mini in the ditch back on the road. . . And there was talk about Alice Taylor." Davy frowned as Dougal and Bob Taylor joined them. "I've not got the whole story, Sergeant. But they say Alice is missing, too."

"That's right, Davy. Have you seen anything?"

Davy scratched his head. "I don't see how Alice can be missing at all."

"Why not?" Bob asked.

"Because I gave her a lift into Auchtarne this morning, on my way back, after dropping Brian Blair and George Locke at the fencing site," said Davy. "She was at the side of the road, carrying a wee bag. . ."

"*You picked up Alice?*" cried Bob, excitedly.

"But no baby?" butted in the Sergeant, quickly.

"Baby? No, of course not. She was carrying just the wee bag."

"Oh, thank God, breathed Bob.

"And you didn't pass that Mini this morning?"

"No. The road was clear—up and down—except for the damn' mists," said Davy.

By this time Wallace had finished talking on the police radio and had joined them.

"Where did you take Alice?" Bob asked.

"Straight into Auchtarne, where she wanted to go. I dropped her by the Auchtarne Hotel, before going on to our depot."

"Alice is sitting in my Surgery," said Wallace, "right now, waiting for me, Bob. Evidently she had decided she wanted to see the Glasgow doctor after all. She wanted his address from me—and a note to him. She'd already been to the railway station to buy a return ticket to Glasgow."

"She didna' tell me any of this," said Bob. "Not a word."

Dougal shrugged. "Be thankit she's safe."

"Aye," said Sergeant Murray, "she's safe, right enough. But what about Moira Moncrieff's wee baby? What's happened to her, eh? Three month old weans canna' get up and walk away by their sel' from a crashed car, can they?" The Sergeant looked up at the sky. The 'break' would soon be over. There were clouds approaching, this time from Ben Darroch way. "Someone took that baby."

"And I'd say," added Dougal, "that they're not on foot, either."

Drew McNair took Moira's trembling hand in both his and squeezed it gently. He could feel the ache in his heart as he looked into her tear-streaked face. And all that shyness was washed away—just as it had been a year ago in her bed at the 'Crawford' in Lanark. He spoke quietly—'nice and carin' and gentle'—as Grace had asked: "We'll find the baby, Moira. Och, you see—we'll find it safe and sound somewhere close by. And after that," said Drew, "you'll come to my home to meet my mother." He smiled apologetically. "It's not a very grand place—bit like the Lachlans' here—but we'll make you welcome."

"Oh, Andy," murmured Moira. He was exactly as she remembered him.

"My mother's alright. You'll like her fine—and she'll tak' to you quick enough, that I can tell." He brought her hand up to his lips. "But you'd better start calling me 'Drew', I think."

Others were still arriving from Glendarroch and Auchtarne. Amongst them was Arthur Chisholm and his
photographer, the latter complaining bitterly about the
failing light. Chisholm told him he knew press photog-
raphers who could have taken group shots in the Black
Hole of Calcutta, if they had been told to. The Reporter
knew he wouldn't get much information from Sergeant
Murray, nor the Factor, for that matter—but there were
men up here, like Tam Shaw, who could talk-up a storm—
if properly prompted. He was sorry that Alice Taylor was
not involved after all. That would have given him a good
angle—'Local Girl Steals Tourist's Baby'—but there was
still a mystery. And a lot of worry. Chisholm thrived on
worry. He took out his notebook, licked the tip of his
pencil and advanced on Tam Shaw, whilst a drumroll of
thunder warned everyone their respite was over.

Elizabeth had not dared to leave the Dower House, despite
Lorna's urgent phone call. Sir Jeffrey would have insisted
that she be driven back to Glendarroch—and if any
newspaper reporter saw that burgundy Rolls-Royce they
would soon sniff out the story. In any case, Mrs Sawyer
was preparing dinner for them, *Carre d'Agneau*, a Crown of
Lamb, quoted Sir Jeffrey, presented with a sauce of honey,
rosemary and mustard. He had a superb Claret, a St Julien,
Chateau Gruaud Larose, Vintage 1962, one of a selection
of special wines packed with tender care in the boot of the
Rolls by Sawyer: Sir Jeffrey proposed they would have it
to complement the lamb.

It would have been churlish for Elizabeth to make an
excuse and forfeit the meal, begging that Estate business
had intruded upon their day together. Sir Jeffrey would
have been bound to contemplate on what urgent chore
could possibly take her away from such a dinner. And
from his company.

12

Echoes through the Rain

Most of the village people and the Estate workers from Glendarroch, who had come up to help in the search, left Ardvain on Sergeant Murray's advice. They left whilst the 'break' still held. Now that Alice had been located, the police really did not know exactly who or what they were looking for—apart from the missing baby. The Factor, the farmers, Archie Menzies, the ghillies, village men and Estate people, all headed back down that road in a long line of slow moving vehicles.

Some stayed. Brian Blair would not leave whilst even the vaguest shadow of suspicion hung over him. The Sergeant's dark hints of suspected violence still rankled him. He would remain until fresh evidence came to light. Hopefully he would be there when they found the baby, safe and well, or had definite news that she was alive. He would be there as a silent reproach to Sergeant Murray He would also be there if the news was bad and the baby was found harmed—or dead. He would be there to try and prove he was innocent and uninvolved. Jimmy stayed with him and sent his two lads back with Archie Menzies in the Factor's Landrover.

Arthur Chisholm remained, of course, bleary-eyed now that the alcoholic euphoria had left him and anxious for this particular story to reach its climax. If the baby was still missing by the morning, then there would be Glasgow newsmen, TV reporters and Camera Crews and his 'exclusive' deal would not be worth a cracker. He had sent off his photographer to the call box below Moncur's to phone in the first draft to his Editor in Auchtarne. And then told him to make a second call to a rewrite-man at the Glasgow press agency with a more detailed, more dramatic story. Arthur Chisholm was completely unhampered by any sense of loyalty to his own newspaper.

Bob Taylor had rushed off much earlier to collect Alice. He had decided they would stay the night at the Auchtarne Hotel and then go on to see the Glasgow psychiatrist next day. He would take her by road. He was delighted that she was, at last, accepting help, even if she had been driven to it only by bleak despair.

Drew McNair stayed with Moira, comforting her the while—'nice and carin' and gentle'—anxious to be with her if any news of Lilian came through: anxious to rediscover the bond that had first drawn him into her arms.

Dr Wallace, exercising that affinity with the Ardvain folk, stayed on, too. He felt the police might need him if the baby was found. It had been missing for over eight hours now.

All the crofters stayed, some of them going out two or three times on different lines, but always returning to report that they had seen nothing. They were certain that there wasn't another living soul, unaccounted for, within a radius of four-and-a-half to five miles from Lachlan's yard. They would keep going over the ground time and time again, however, to ensure that they had missed nothing. Those who lived closest had their womenfolk organise hot food for the rest. Willie Tulloch's wife made five journeys back to their croft for food.

Others had come up to Ardvain. Ken Calder had been asked by the police to drag Moira's Mini out of the ditch and tow it back to the Auchtarne Police Station for closer examination. Ken felt particularly distressed when he heard about the accident. If it had been caused by some mechanical failure than perhaps he ought to accept some responsibility for the events that had occurred. Maybe he should have checked the car out more thoroughly.

The Auchtarne Police Inspector arrived, but he kept a very low profile. He received Sergeant Murray's report and did not presume to offer advice or further instructions. The Inspector was very much aware of the fact that he was new in the area and very much a city policeman, anyway. Even Auchtarne had felt like the middle of nowhere after the streets of Glasgow. Ardvain was a wilderness.

Overhead the RAF helicopter made wide, slow circles in the sky, taking advantage of every minute of the 'break'. But, like everyone else the pilot did not know what he was looking for.

And the news of the baby's disappearance was reported in the early BBC radio bulletin. Ardvain and Glendarroch were now sharing their turmoil with the rest of the world. Fortunately, by then, Alice's suspected involvement was not mentioned.

Fortunately, too, there were no radios switched on at the Dower House, where Sir Jeffrey and Elizabeth were having their pre-dinner aperitifs. He was watching her very carefully. Perhaps it was just his imagination, but he thought she seemed just a little nervous, a little less relaxed now than she had been earlier in the day. She had appeared just a fraction ill at ease ever since that phone call from Glendarroch House.

Two others were still out on Ardvain. Alec Geddes and Fiona Cunningham were away on their second search, moving slower this time and zig-zagging so that they could scan even more ground as they rode. Their horses were getting tired now and both riders and mounts were soaked and muddy. They had taken a northwesterly line and had travelled some seven and a half miles from Lachlan's cottage, farther afield than anyone else on foot had been.

Now they both dismounted and were walking Tamberlaine and Belair, taking advantage of the 'break' and able to converse without having to shout at the top of their voices. Steam was billowing from the flanks of the horses and even from their own waterproof anoraks, but there would be no time for them or their horses to dry out before the storm overtook them again.

Fiona was supposed to be leading the way—Geddes was a relative newcomer to the Estate—but Tamberlaine had been very nervous of the thunder and lightning and she had fought to control him, consequently much of her attention just before the 'break' had been focussed on keeping herself in the saddle, rather than on the direction they were taking. So when the 'break' came she had to admit that she was lost—but only temporarily, she assured Geddes.

"We could walk in circles for hours up here, Fiona," said Geddes, angrily, "and then they'll have to send that damn' 'copter out to search for us!"

"God, but you're a bright ray of sunshine, aren't you?" She was quite unconcerned. She knew that sooner or later she would see a recognisable landmark and then know exactly where she was. After all, she was a Peddie, wasn't she? This would have been her land, her heritage—if Death Duties had not intervened and deprived her of it all. She had spent a great deal of time up on Ardvain in days gone by—with her grandfather, the old Laird, and her mother and, best of all, with crofters like Dougal Lachlan and Jamie Lockhart and Willie Tulloch, dour men under a roof, but alive and full of knowledge up here. "I'd say we were on Willie Tulloch's land."

"Oh, yes, no mistaking it," said Geddes, his voice heavy with sarcasm, "you can tell that by the different shade of purple worn by his heather!"

"Yes, it *is* Willie Tulloch's land!" beamed Fiona, triumphantly. "Here's the old distillery road." She hurried on, dragging Tamberlaine after her, and came to a well-defined, though deep-rutted track, still easily visible through the gorse and heather. It was a track that once, long ago, had been quite a busy thoroughfare.

Geddes joined her and stared down at the bare clay. "Distillery road?" he said.

"That's right. We had our own distillery on the Estate when my great-grandfather was still alive. 'Glendarroch Malt'. It was much sought after, I might tell you, by folk who knew their whiskies. Though my mother says that the majority of it never left my great-grandfather's cellars. He was something of a connoisseur of the old *uisge-beatha*. Either that—or he was a bit of a soak. Probably both. Anyway, the distillery closed down just after he died. It's down there a couple of miles, but it's only a shell now. No one's used this track for years. . ."

"Someone has," said Geddes. He bent down to examine some churned mud and saw the multi-hued stain of oil floating on the surface of a puddle. "Quite recently. Maybe today." He pointed to the freshly broken stem of a gorse shrub. "And they had trouble getting along here, too. They did a bit of skidding about in the mud. It was a car or a small truck, but not a four-wheel drive. Where does the track lead to after the distillery?"

"Nowhere. It's a dead end."

"And the other way?"

"It joins the Ardvain road, just past Tulloch's croft."

There was a thunderclap, much nearer than those warning them earlier that the storm was coming back.

Tamberlaine stomped at the ground and flared his nostrils in fear.

"I think we must go there and investigate, Fiona," said Geddes. He looked down the track to the crest of a slope that hid the abandoned distillery from view. "Two miles, you reckon?"

"Or three," said Fiona. "Depends on where we are on the track." She shrugged apologetically. "No more than three, anyway."

"You want me to take Tamberlaine?"

"No, he'll be better this time." She looked up at the sky and the first drop of rain fell onto the peak of her riding hat. Geddes gave her a leg up as her horse whinnied nervously. Then he mounted Belair and together they broke into a steady, mile-eating trot alongside the track leading to the derelict buildings that had once been the home of 'Glendarroch Malt Whisky'.

"No," said the Sergeant, shaking his head slowly, "it's not really Brian Blair's style at all. That's if he's got a style. He only had that one conviction, you know, sir. He has no other record." Murray was sitting in the police car with the Inspector. They were both staring through the windscreen at Jimmy and Brian sitting in their van just a few yards from them, sheltering from the rain that was filtering down now from the leaden skies. The clouds had materialised from nowhere. The 'break' was over. "He killed a woman in a fit of uncontrollable temper. Spur of the moment homicide, crime of passion. I don't see why Blair would want to kill a baby."

"I'm sure you're right, Sergeant," agreed the Inspector. He firmly believed he was wasting his time here. The baby was, he thought, either dead and already buried somewhere in this awesome wilderness, in which case they would never find the tiny body, or else the child had been abducted by someone in a vehicle, for some reason, and was perhaps north of Oban by now or south of Carlisle. The situation had already been reported to Glasgow and very soon now the Inspector thought they would send the big-wigs up from the city and the responsibility would be taken from his shoulders. He glanced at the Sergeant. The man was wearing a perpetual frown, squinting his eyes as though trying to find a path through a bank of dense fog. "Lived in the area all your life, Sergeant?" he asked.

"Aye, born and bred in Auchtarne, Sir. Did a stint in Gourock a long while back, but this has been my patch most of the time." His thumb and forefinger crept back to tug at the lobe of his ear again. "And you, sir? Where do you hail from? Are you a Glaswegian, born and bred?"

"More or less, though I went to school in Kelso. . ."

And suddenly that was it! From the most unlikely source had come the answer—not even directly, but in a devious, tortuous route. That elusive point, the thing that had eluded him, the name—it now stood out as though lit up by neon lights! He pulled so hard on the lobe of his ear that it made him grunt with pain as he yelled: "*Kelso!*"

The Inspector looked at him, startled. "Yes, Kelso," he said.

"Kelso is in *Roxburgh*!!" said Murray, excitedly. "Roxburgh!" he repeated. "That's it!" The Sergeant opened the door of the car and bellowed for Jimmy Blair. He and his father came running over.

"What is it, Sergeant?" asked Jimmy, anxiously.

"That lass you said you were dating, y'ken? Jeannie Roxburgh—that's the name you said?"

"Aye?"

And the light went on for the Inspector, too. "Oh, my God," he said. "Jeannie Roxburgh. . ."

"What about her?" asked Brian.

"Get in the back of the car, both of you," said the Sergeant. "You'll get soaked out there." His mind was churning over now, putting all those tangled threads together, as Brian and Jimmy got into the back seat.

"Are we going to need a lawyer?" asked Brian, suspiciously, whilst he slammed the door behind them. Sitting in the back seat of a police car brought back too many painful memories. Jimmy could almost feel his father's fear mounting.

"Just shut up the two of you, whilst I sort this out," said the Sergeant.

"Where the hell was it, Sergeant?" the Inspector asked, racking his own brain. "Where was it?"

"Dumbarton, last time. Two years ago. Before that it was Troon in Ayrshire."

"What are you talking about?" said Jimmy, leaning forward.

But Murray ignored him for the moment. The whole thing was like some ghastly jigsaw puzzle, all falling into place. "Only daughter of a rich father, Maxwell A. Roxburgh, industrialist, shipping, I think," said the Sergeant, reeling it off, pulling the information out of the filing cabinet of his memory. He spoke over his shoulder to Jimmy: "Your girlfriend Jeannie—does she have plenty of money, Jimmy?"

"Aye, she had a quid or two, I suppose. . ."

"Father put her into an expensive Psychiatric Nursing Home, near Drymen," the Sergeant went on, "discharged as mentally fit and reasonable after Troon. Then again after Dumbarton, I'll wager! Her mother died in an asylum when she was very young and she was brought up by a succession of Nannies and Nurses—a very disturbed childhood, so the papers said."

"Are you still talking about Jeannie, Sergeant?" asked Jimmy, totally confused.

"Blonde lass, Jimmy, full lips, grey eyes?"

"Aye, that's her. . ."

"Then I'm still talking about her, lad."

The Inspector was already speaking into the radio, relaying this new information through to Glasgow and his Divisional Commander.

"What did she do?" asked Brian.

"She stole other people's babies—and she ran off with them," said the Sergeant. "She treated them as make-believe dolls. Unfortunately, when she got bored with them—she ditched them. Or tried to. Luckily the Dumbarton baby was found in the back of her car—in the boot—wrapped in newspaper, but alive and squawking fit to bust." He paused for a moment to take a breath. "The Troon baby, a little girl, too, was not so lucky. They found her after three days—also wrapped in newspaper—but in a dustbin. The poor mite was dead." The Sergeant leaned forward, opened the glove locker and brought out a large scale map of the immediate area. "Suffocation, they said. Jeannie was charged. They got halfway through the case— then the doctors said she was mentally unbalanced. It was written up in great detail in all the newspapers."

"Jesus," whispered Brian, "that bonny lass? That lovely creature. . .?" Jimmy was too stunned to say anything. He just stared—and remembered Jeannie's perfect body—and then recalled those strange dead-grey eyes that only sometimes smouldered.

"Where was she staying, Jimmy?" asked Murray.

"What?"

"Where was she staying in Glendarroch?"

"I don't know. . . A bed and breakfast place—somewhere on the Auchtarne Road. . .," Jimmy answered vaguely.

"Lay you odds of five-to-one it was Molly Mac-Phearson's place. And that's where Moira Moncrieff and her baby stayed, too! So Jeannie would have seen the wean and known that Moira was going up to Ardvain." The Sergeant felt his mouth go taut. "It fits. Oh, my God, it all fits—and I should've seen it a couple of hours ago." Now he turned in his seat to face the anguished Jimmy. "Tell me about her car, lad: what was she drivin'?"

"Sports car," said Jimmy, dully. "White TR7—you know —yon wedge-shaped jobs. I think she had it souped up—it revved like a motorbike. . ."

The Sergeant quoted Moira's words to him: " '. . .a *giant ray*—like a great *sheet*. . . roarin'—and comin' straight at me!' That's what she told me. The bonnet of a white TR7 coming at you through a fog patch, could look like a sheet—or a giant ray, couldn't it? And it was roarin'!" The Sergeant looked to Jimmy for confirmation. "The bonnet of a TR7—it's flat, isn't it? Hers was flat and white."

Jimmy nodded mutely. Brian squeezed his son's arm.

The Sergeant turned back to his Inspector. "Jeannie Roxburgh never took the babies far away. She drove them in her car only a few miles each time. In Dumbarton it was a car park. In Troon it was a quiet street only three miles from where she took the baby."

"You think she may be near by?" asked the Inspector.

"I may even be able to pinpoint her, sir!" Sergeant Murray opened up the map and traced his finger along the thin line of the Ardvain road. "Willie Tulloch said he thought he heard someone using a chainsaw behind his place. Jamie Stewart said he heard nothing —but Jamie's a wee bit deaf. There's an old track running behind Tulloch's croft and right across his land. It leads to an old derelict distillery building, no more than a shell, but the waggon shed has a roof still on it, as I recall. You could hide a car in there."

"And her car was souped," said Jimmy. "It revved like a motorbike. If she was skidding a wee bit those revs might sound like—a chain-saw, maybe. . ."

"Well, let's have a look," said the Inspector, praying that Sergeant Murray had made the break-through, praying that he might be right, praying that they might be in time. "We'll need to take Dr Wallace with us—thank goodness he's still here."

"I'm afraid it's because of this sort of eventuality," said the Sergeant, "that he *is* still here."

They got out of the car. They would travel up to the old distillery in a police Range Rover—and in a four-wheel drive all the way.

Jimmy and Brian stayed in the back seat for a while. Jimmy very much doubted if his legs would hold him if he tried to stand. He felt sick—and incredulous at the same time. She was waiting round that bend for Moira and her little baby? Jeannie Roxburgh? Yet now, when he thought about it carefully—there was always something that disturbed him about those grey, dead eyes. And that frantic need of hers to love—and be loved.

13

Storm's Finale

The rain was pelting down again, whipped almost horizontal by the biting wind, as Alec Geddes and Fiona rode up to the old distillery.

Here the track they were following split into two. One arm led to the Pot Stills round the back of the building, the other straight into the waggon shed, where the horse drawn barley carts used to discharge their loads for the first screenings. Over to their left was the once tiny burn from where the all-important water was drawn. Now, in this weather, it was engorged and rushing like a frothing conveyor belt gone mad.

They could see the back of the white Triumph TR7 sports car parked in the doorless waggon shed and Alec signalled Fiona to dismount. The noise of the storm would drown any sound they made, but they might be seen through the car's rear vision mirror. They moved to one side. Alec took Tamberlaine's rein and walked the horses to the lee of the building, where he found a ringbolt set into the stone beside an arch, and tethered them there.

He beckoned Fiona to him and spoke close to her ear. "You recognise that car?"

Fiona nodded. "Yes. Belongs to that girl who came up to the stables to question me about Jimmy. She was a bit keen on him, I think. Wanted to warn me off. Odd type, I thought. Easy on the eye, though—if you care for that sort of thing." And she gave Alec a quizzical little grin, despite the fact that her face was streaming with rain water. "Her name was Jeannie Roxburgh, she said."

"What the hell is she doing up here?"

"I daren't think, Alec!"

"We'll have to find out. But I don't want to scare her off. Do you know if there's another way into that shed?"

She nodded and pointed to a small door just beyond the horses. "Leads past the malting floor and into the back of the waggon shed," she said, straining to make herself heard above the din of the weather.

"You'd better stay here . . ." began Geddes.

"No, Alec. I think I ought to make the first contact with

her somehow. I've got a feeling she's not alone in there,"
said Fiona.

"The baby?"

"I don't know—but I'd say she was hiding, wouldn't
you?"

They went in through the door and across the roofless
malting floor. Even before they were halfway to the
entrance of the shed—even over the din of the storm—
they heard a baby crying lustily.

They moved in quietly and saw that the car was empty.

Jeannie Roxburgh was sitting in a dark corner of the
shed, crouched as small as she could get, knees drawn up
and rocking steadily to and fro. In her arms, and clutched
tightly to her chest, was a white bundle. And it was from
this bundle that the crying came.

"Don't frighten her," said Geddes in a hushed voice.
"For God's sake don't frighten her. She's holding the baby
too tight!"

They moved closer and Geddes put a restraining hand
on Fiona's arm. But she gently tugged herself free and
walked towards the huddled figure. "Jeannie," she called
very softly, yet somehow making her voice carry over the
noise of the baby and the storm outside. "Jeannie," Fiona
repeated.

And Jeannie raised her head slowly and looked straight
at Fiona. Those dead grey eyes seemed alive now, almost
as though they were animated by tiny electric sparks. That
glorious blonde hair was in disarray and hung about her
shoulders, down her back and across her face in thick,
limp straggles. "No, Nanny!" shouted Jeannie, suddenly.
"No, Nanny! This is my doll! I'm keeping this one. You
mustn't throw this dolly away!" And she propelled herself
upwards against the corner, until she was standing,
defiantly, still clutching Lilian tightly to her chest. "No,
Nanny! You just keep away! You can't have this dolly! I
won't let you!"

"Oh, God," said Geddes, "she's out of her head!"

But Fiona continued to move forward, instinctively
adapting herself to the situation. "It's alright, Jeannie. I'm
not going to take your dolly away," she said. "I just want to
have a look at it . . ."

It was then that Jeannie screamed very loudly, turned to

one side and dashed from the shed—and into the screeching storm outside. She ran very fast, still holding Lilian,
but with the rain pounding at them both—and Fiona and
Geddes just a yard or two behind, slithering in their riding
boots until they got into their stride.

Jeannie was running for the stream, the burn that was
now an angry, dangerous torrent. And a terrible sense of
dread seized Fiona.

The light was going, too. The darkness would quickly
roll over the storm-lashed landscape now as the night
hurried towards them.

And in Fiona's ears a score of different sounds, orch-
estrating into a terrible cacophany: the bass-drum
percussion of the thunder, the tympanic tattoo of the rain,
Jeannie's howl of mad misery, Lilian's gulping cries, the
terror-filled whinnies of Tamberlaine as lightning illuminated everything for a few micro-seconds—and the
ominous roar of that small stream, frothing and churning
in flooded fury along the confines of its narrow rock-sided
gorge . . .

Then Geddes cursed loudly as his foot caught in the
thick tendril of a trailing briar and he went down heavily.
But he saw that Fiona was gaining on Jeannie. As he
scrambled to his feet he saw, too, behind them, coming
along the track, the bright eyes of car headlights . . .

Jeannie had reached the edge of the stream and was
standing on a flat stone overhang, a curtain of spray
spewing up excitedly around her. She turned to face Fiona,
teeth bared now, snarling. "No, you shan't have my dolly!"
she screamed, raising the tiny bundle above her head. But
Fiona's own momentum carried her forward. She grabbed
at Lilian and dragged the baby into her own arms, using
her hip to push Jeannie away, gasping with relief at the
close call.

The baby was safe and Fiona turned quickly and ran
back, fearing that the crazed girl would come after her.
However, Geddes was running past, making for that
overhang—because he had seen Jeannie Roxburgh topple
slowly, so slowly that he thought he might reach her
before she went into the torrent below. Even as that image
was imprinted in his mind—she disappeared from view.
Geddes saw that straggle of hair break through the froth

for a moment before he dived into the cauldron after her. Under the spume the swirling water was brown and peaty and paralysingly cold. The force buffeted Geddes, twisting his body round and round. Then his outstretched hands caught Jeannie's shoulder and he held on tight as she fought him like a drowning wildcat. He could feel his riding boots hampering him, but they were too tight to shake off . . .

After what seemed an eternity to him, the sheer sides of rock gave way to a sodden bank and Geddes dragged the now limp body of Jeannie to it. She was alive and retching with the amount of water she had swallowed, but the fight had gone from her and, maybe for a while, so had the madness. She was like a bedraggled child, doll-like herself, with dull, expressionless smokey grey eyes. She neither helped nor hindered Geddes as he hauled her from the water. She just looked confused and puzzled, as though she wondered where she was—and how she had got there.

In the background Geddes could see a hazy picture of Fiona, with the baby in her arms, running towards him anxiously, her figure lit up by the headlights of two police Range Rovers and a couple of the crofters' vehicles behind them.

The wine in Arthur Chisholm's stomach had long since turned to vinegar and the acid felt as though it was burning his gut with a white-hot flame. He was in a foul mood.

He knew he had been cheated with this story. They had found the missing kid too quickly—it had barely been gone ten hours. Of course, it had a bit of drama and a good climax, the Jeannie Roxburgh involvement was a bonus, the setting for the 'rescue' was unique—but it was all one-off stuff. It was one rattling good article—and then—finish. Maybe a next day follow-up, but that was all. Ideally what Arthur Chisholm had been looking for was a long, tension-filled search, lasting maybe three or four days—with good juicy, rewarding progress reports in every edition. That would have been worth real money to him.

In the meantime, he was getting no cooperation from anyone. Geddes was a dour, untalkative devil. Sergeant Murray had a healthy dislike for the press and of being referred to the Police Press Liason Officer—who was nowhere near the scene, anyway. And Dr Wallace seemed too busy to spare him even a minute or give him a quote.

However, the baby was well and Chisholm's photographer had snatched a good shot of mother and child being re-united, though Chisholm wondered what the hell Drew McNair was doing still hanging around the place. The crofter even went with Moira and Lilian in the ambulance when it came to take them down to the Auchtarne Cottage Hospital. Even the baby seemed little the worse for its experience: 'hardy wee creatures', Chisholm had heard Wallace mutter.

Dougal Lachlan's yard, which only an hour or two ago had been full of people, was now almost empty. Tam Shaw, the reporter's fount of all knowledge, had been one of the first to head home after the baby was found. And Chisholm missed getting a photo of Jeannie Roxburgh as the police bustled her away. He wondered if it wouldn't have made a better story if Alice Taylor *had* stolen the kid .

It was dark now, they had that blasted road to negotiate back and the storm was still belting away. Chisholm felt as though his head would split open with the racket. He was not a happy man.

He decided he would get the tail-piece for his story from Fiona Cunningham—and he'd pull out every cliche he could from the keys of his typewriter. If necessary he would make her the heroine of the piece—the housewives loved classy heroines with a bit of upper-crust panache to them . . . 'Laird's Grand-daughter Grabs Baby From the Brink of Death'—something like that, anyway.

Trouble was that in the general exodus he and his photographer had missed Fiona.

Arthur Chisholm's temper was not improving. Like the weather, his great and lucrative story was proving to be something of a washout.

Willie Tulloch had stabled Tamberlaine and Belair in his barn. Sometime tomorrow Geddes would send a man up from his farm to collect the horse box from Moncur's, take it up to Tulloch's and bring the two horses back.

Fiona and Geddes had travelled back in Tulloch's Landrover with Sergeant Murray and had given the policeman a full statement of all that had happened. Geddes told his story in between sneezes, much to the consternation of Fiona, who had insisted he wrap himself in one of the blankets they found in the back of the Landrover. It smelt very strongly of sheep and sheep-dip.

Jeannie Roxburgh travelled in more comfort, wrapped in cleaner, police issue blankets, in the police Range Rover, with the Inspector. She was very subdued now—and spoke not at all.

And Wallace looked after the baby in the Inveraray police Range Rover. Grace Lachlan, hoping desperately that they would find Lilian safe and sound, though perhaps a little damp, had given Wallace blankets and woollies that Donald had worn—and she had, sentimentally, saved. She also thought to provide a thermos of warm, diluted milk and a baby's bottle. Lilian had lain, warm and contented, in Wallace's arms, sucking sleepily at the bottle.

There were cheers as the tiny convoy drove into Dougal's yard and the crofters ignored the teeming rain and hailed Fiona and Geddes as the heroes of the day, much to the latter's annoyance and embarrassment.

Jimmy was around, waiting to see Jeannie, but she wasn't there long. They transferred her from the Range Rover to the police car—and as she walked over to it, Jimmy broke away from his father and ran to her. "Jeannie," he shouted, "I'm sorry. I'm awfy sorry." She turned, looked at him, smiled and waved. It was impossible for him to tell whether she recognised him or not.

Then Brian was at his shoulder. "Come on, son, let's go on home now. Your mother will be worryin'."

They watched as Jeannie was helped into the back seat of the car by the Inspector. She looked forlorn and vulnerable. She did not look back as the car drove away.

"It could have been my fault, Dad," Jimmy said. "She wanted to go away with me—och, just for a couple of days . . . I said 'no'. I knocked her back. I mean, it could've been my fault, eh?" He watched the tail lights of the receding police car until they vanished from view. "I could've been—kinder—maybe. But I had no idea she was . . . she was ill." He nodded slowly. "I could've still been kinder."

Together they walked over to the van. The Sergeant was there. There was no sense in ignoring him. "We'll be away now, Sergeant," said Brian, "if it's alright with you."

"Aye, it's alright," said Murray. He opened the passenger door for Brian. "Gave you bad time, did I?"

"What do you think?" said Brian, sourly.

"I'm not going to apologise. It'll always be that way, I'm afraid. Anything bad that happens on this patch—and my thoughts will turn to you, immediately." He closed the van door as Brian settled himself in the seat and clicked on his safety belt.

Brian wound down the window. "It's nice to feel needed, Sergeant," he said.

The Sergeant laughed. "Go on," he said, "get on back to Isabel. I expect your family need you a hell of a lot more than I do, eh, Brian?"

Brian looked at his son. "Aye, I expect they do."

The Sergeant turned and walked towards the door of Lachlan's croft as Jimmy drove the van away from the yard.

It was, Elizabeth Cunningham decided, a quite magical meal—despite the nagging worry that tugged at her. She knew Lorna Seton would not ring again, unless the situation up on Ardvain became absolutely desperate. She hoped they had found the police had gone—and taken any stray newspapermen with them. She hoped, devoutly, that all was peaceful out there—especially now that the storm had finally blown itself out.

She hoped it was peaceful, but she had no way of knowing.

There were apologies from Mrs Sawyer, because she was not used to the stove, she said, though Elizabeth could find absolutely no fault whatsoever with the lamb. The wine was as mellow and as silky as Sir Jeffrey had hoped, the table was a delight to the eye, the silverware gleaming, the glasses sparkling. The Dower House dining room had, in Elizabeth's view, never looked lovelier. She had, of course, dined there many, many times through the course of her life, but no meal had been quite like this. Dowager Aunts and Grandmothers did not entertain in this fashion.

Sawyer left them with an abundant coffee pot and their cognac. And the time just glided away. However, it had been a very full day for them and as the clock struck eleven Elizabeth, very reluctantly, brought the evening to an end.

"I'll ring through to my daughter to come and pick me up," she said. Elizabeth did not have her car at the Dower House.

"You will do no such thing, dear lady," said Sir Jeffrey. "If you are absolutely determined to leave, then it will be our pleasure to drive you home. If I am supremely fortunate, I may even be invited in for a final cup of coffee."

Elizabeth felt a tremble of panic. She had no idea what they would see between here and Glendarroch House. Police cars were white, they stood out in the dark. "There really is no need, Jeffrey," she said. They had dispensed with the 'Sir' just after the Rainbow Trout and the last glass of Pouilly Fuisse. "Fiona will still be wide awake and . . ."

"I insist," he said. "Sawyer has the car at the front door—whenever you are ready."

They saw nothing, absolutely nothing, as the Rolls drifted through the night and through the village towards the House; no police cars, no sign of anxious villagers waiting for news—nothing.

"I am sorry, Mr Chisholm," Fiona said, "but I am desperately tired, it's eleven o'clock, and I have the bath running. Now, if you'll excuse me . . ." And she began to shut the door on Arthur Chisholm, who now felt as though the entire world was in league against him.

"Just a round-off for my newspaper, Miss Cunningham," he pleaded. "A tail-piece."

"You'll get no 'tail-piece' here," said Fiona. She couldn't help grinning at the inference, however.

"Could I ring tomorrow?"

"Yes. Do that. I'll speak to you tomorrow," promised Fiona. "I'll give you all the lurid details then."

"Lurid?" asked Chisholm, hopefully.

"Just joking, Mr Chisholm. Just joking. Goodnight now."

"Tomorrow, then?"

"Yes," said Fiona. She really was tired and she could hear the bath water still running. She longed to be soaking in its warmth.

Chisholm was very persistent. He had just thought of something. "Perhaps I could speak to Mrs Cunningham. I noticed she wasn't up on Ardvain . . ."

"My mother is not in"

"Oh?"

"I think she has a dinner engagement."

"Ah."

"Goodnight, *Mr* Chisholm!" And Fiona shut the door hard.

Chisholm pulled a face, turned and walked down the long, sweeping staircase, to the hall below. He had never been inside Glendarroch House in the old days when the whole of it had been a private home for the one family. He had never covered the 'social scene' for his paper when the old Laird was alive. He glanced at the doors that led to the Factor's Office and the Reception area. There were no lights on underneath. The place was quite dead. He wondered why Elizabeth Cunningham, the 'Lady Laird', as some folk called her, had not been up on Ardvain? What pressing engagement could have kept her from being there—with her 'people'? It was odd. He would need to find out, he decided.

As Chisholm opened the front door the big burgundy coloured Rolls-Royce drove up and parked quietly at the steps.

And then, for Arthur Chisholm, belicose, cynical reporter for the 'Auchtarne Gazette', the whole world suddenly began to shine with a golden glow, despite the surrounding blackness of the night! The sour wine that still sloshed in his belly became soothing milk and his head cleared miraculously in a split second.

Just beneath him, and in clear view, he watched as Elizabeth Cunningham got out of the car, courteously assisted by Sir Jeffrey Leighton-Fyffe, banker and financial adviser supreme. Immediately Chisholm's brain moved into overdrive.

He knew, as did everyone else locally, that Glendarroch Estates had a 'cash-flow' and a 'profitability' problem that were a perpetual drain on the Frankfurt multi-national that owned the place. The Meier Corporation, Chisholm was certain, would undoubtedly be interested in any possible offer to buy them out.

He also *knew* and immediately *recognised* Sir Jeffrey, even though the banker rarely gave press interviews.

Chisholm had been doing some freelance work in Stirling years ago, he couldn't even remember the name of the rag that was employing him at the time, but he could remember everything else. He had been called to cover the rather sordid death of a woman in a remote hotel near the Bridge of Allen—a woman who had killed herself with an overdose of drugs. She had been identified as Lady Jane Leighton-Fyffe. Chisholm was there when the husband, Sir Jeffrey, arrived to take her body away. He had spoken to him, he had even got a couple of quotes from him. Chisholm would never ever forget Sir Jeffrey—and he had followed the banker's career from that moment on. He knew almost everything about his work.

He knew, for instance, that Sir Jeffrey was the financial adviser to a certain Trade Union Pension Fund—one of the richest in the country—even though it was as Left Wing as any could be without actually flying the hammer and sickle from its office window.

Sir Jeffrey—the Pension Fund—Glendarroch Estate. Oh, what a beautiful story! The militant Union investing its many millions in this monument to privilege—buying out Frankfurt, perhaps? Was that it?

It was as they began climbing those first steps to the front door that Sir Jeffrey and Elizabeth saw Chisholm. The reporter was positively beaming. "Sir Jeffrey Leighton-Fyffe?" he said, taking his notebook from his pocket. "I don't suppose you remember me? My name's Chisholm and I'm a journalist for the *Auchtarne Gazette*—may I ask what brings you to Glendarroch, sir?" And Chisholm waved frantically to his photographer, who, up until that moment, had been cat-napping. The young man grabbed his camera and flash-gun, jumped out of his car, and ran towards the group.

Sir Jeffrey's face had suddenly set hard. The eyes narrowed, the lips became a thin line. "I am here visiting my good friend, Mrs Cunningham. Now, if you'll excuse us . . ." He moved on up the steps and was beside the front door, with Elizabeth on his right, when the photographer clicked his camera and the flash went off. It was no accident that Sir Jeffrey was standing right beside the brass nameplate that proclaimed: 'Glendarroch Estate Limited—Factor's Office and Enquiries'. Elizabeth felt her heart sink.

"Not here on business, then, sir?" asked Chisholm.

"I've just told you what I'm doing here!" said Sir Jeffrey, his voice ice-clear and controlled.

"Lot of Pension Funds investing in land these days, sir," said the reporter, far too casually.

"Is that so?"

"What about the Fund you represent, sir? Would they be at all interested in Glendarroch Estate? As an investment?"

Sir Jeffrey turned to Elizabeth. She could see the look of regret in his eyes as he answered: "No, Mr Chisholm. No, they would not."

And she knew it was over.

However, Chisholm would not let it lie. "The rumour is that Frankfurt would be willing to take any reasonable offer."

"I am not here to invest in this Estate, Mr Chisholm," Sir Jeffrey said, most definitely. "And if you print anything to the contrary, I shall take legal action. There are fundamental differences in ideology between those who subscribe to the Pension Fund I represent and the feudal structure of an Estate such as this. Those ideologies could never be reconciled to each other." He gave Chisholm a withering look. "You may print *that*, if you wish, Mr Chisholm." Sir Jeffrey took Elizabeth's hand and kissed it very gently. "Goodnight, Elizabeth. Thank you for a thoroughly enchanting day." He looked directly into her eyes. "Perhaps I'll come back again next summer, if I may?"

"I hope you will," Elizabeth said. "Maybe the weather will be kinder then."

He bowed to her, almost imperceptibly: a secret gesture of respect from a Gallant to his Ladye. Then he turned, ignoring Chisholm completely, and walked to the Rolls, where Sawyer was waiting with the rear passenger door open. Sir Jeffrey got inside.

"Mrs Cunningham," said Chisholm, undeterred, "I wonder if I might just . . ."

"I wonder," she said to him, "if you wouldn't mind going straight to hell, Mr Chisholm."

Sir Jeffrey's car swung round and purred away.

Elizabeth opened the front door and slammed it behind her. Chisholm heard the bolt on the other side rammed home viciously.

"Well?" said the photographer.

But the reporter was far too concerned with his stomach to answer. The wine had turned sour once more and he could feel the sledge-hammers pounding in his head again.

14

The Same View from Laird's Vantage

It was still her favourite place. She could still build her fairytales and fantasies here, even though she knew demons continued to lurk in the mists below and Teutonic dragons remained close by.

But there *had* been a knight in shining armour and he had ridden by on a fine burgundy coloured horse. Unfortunately, he had not stayed long enough to fight any monsters, nor joust with any dragons. However, he might return next summer. Might ride by again, perhaps when there were fewer storm clouds threatening.

There had been some 'Happy Ever Afters', though.

Moira Moncrieff and her little daughter, Lilian, were living at the McNair croft and it was rumoured that Drew's mother seemed very fond of her.

Alice Taylor looked less wan, a little less haunted. Perhaps her regular trips to that doctor in Glasgow were beginning to benefit her. Certainly Bob Taylor seemed much more optimistic these days. And there was talk of wee Donald Lachlan returning to the Taylor cottage. Dougal, Grace and Morag would miss him, of course, but it wasn't as though it was far away.

Brian Blair had a contract with the Forestry for six weeks work. It would be hard work, of course, but he was delighted to have it. He held his head a little higher these days and Isabel smiled more often.

As for the other side of things . . .

Well, Jimmy Blair would take some time to put Jeannie Roxburgh out of his mind, but Elizabeth thought he might be over it by next summer, when the Aqua Sports started up again.

Her own daughter, Fiona, and Alec Geddes? Nothing had changed there. She was still totally infatuated by him. It gave Mrs Mack and Murdoch an awful lot to talk and tut-tut about . . .

She looked down at Glendarroch House and tried to remember how delightful the surrounding lawns had been long ago. It was hard to imagine them as they were when her father was alive—bright green and velvet smooth.

Now Archie Menzies had put away the cutters until next spring, even though the grass would still grow for a while before the winter set in.

Archie Menzies? Always so nervous whenever Moira Moncrieff came to the village. Very strange. Elizabeth had heard her call him 'Wayne Forrester'. Maybe she had mistaken him for someone else. Or was it true about those trips to Lanark—and how all the Glendarroch and Ardvain men never used their real names in the pubs? But 'Wayne Forrester'—really! No wonder he was embarrassed. Elizabeth wondered if he had fixed that scullery window pane round the back. She very much doubted it.

Ironically, the sky was bright and clear today. Not a cloud anywhere. Sir Jeffrey should have seen Glendarroch on a day such as this. She could have brought him up here and he would have seen how much closer Ardvain appeared from the Vantage—and how the River Darroch twisted its way down from up there, like a ribbon of pure silver in the sunlight.

She loved this place. She would always come here. Always. Regardless of what the future might hold for any of them.

It was all very beautiful—and very sad sometimes.

At least, that was the view she got from Laird's Vantage.